Demise of the Undertaker's Wife
A Short Story Collection

Anne Walsh Donnelly

Demise of the Undertaker's Wife
A Short Story Collection

Anne Walsh Donnelly

Dedicated to my loving parents,
Winne and Tom Walsh

Thanks

Thanks to my mother, (especially for bringing me to the local library every week when I was a child and fostering my love of reading) and to my father, (from whom I've inherited my story-telling ability). Thanks also to my five brothers for their encouragement and support.

Sincere gratitude to the Blue Nib team and Dave Kavanagh, for their editorial input and all their hard work in bringing this collection to publication.

Thanks to Claire Loader for allowing me to use her photo of *Meadow of Graves, Inishmore, County Galway.*

Thanks to all those who read and gave valuable feedback on some of these stories. Thanks to the various writing groups I have been privileged to be a part of over the years, especially the GMIT Mayo creative writing class of 2013, the Museum writers group and Poets Abroad.

Special thanks to Mai O'Neill for encouraging me to start and continue writing.

The biggest thanks of all go to my two children, Brian and Hannah, for their constant love and acceptance of all my endeavors and for trying not to disturb me when I am in the 'writing zone.'

Acknowledgements

I wish to acknowledge the publications in which some of these stories or versions of them, originally appeared; Cránnog, Henshaw Two Anthology, Ireland's Own Anthology, Creative Writing Ink Journal, Writer's Forum and The Blue Nib Magazine

Contents

Goodbye, Mr. Fox

The kitchen window creaks as Luke pushes it open. He sticks his head out, sucks in the morning air. It's laced with the smell of the wretched fox that won't leave his hens alone. They don't give him eggs anymore, but that's no reason to let the fox take them, he thinks. Aren't they entitled to live out the rest of their days in peace like he should be, instead of being evicted from his home? Luke squints as he searches the field nearest the house for a smudge of red fur. He's there; Luke feels it in his bones.

Damien's Land Rover comes rattling up the lane. Luke jumps back from the window, the mug of tea in his hand flies and lands in the fireplace where the remains of last night's turf lie. Only a minute before he'd stoked it for the smell of the peat smoke that evokes the picture of Walter in his mind.

The squeal of the rusty hinge on the door of the Land Rover drags Luke to the window again. He watches Damien march to the whitethorn ditch with the 'For Sale' sign and his sledge hammer. Luke strokes the week-old stubble covering his jowls. He'd hoped after yesterday that Damien would change his mind. He flinches as the hammer pounds the stake. Walter's sheepdog yelps in the yard.

Luke grabs the shotgun from the top of the kitchen dresser, pushes the back door open and steps onto the dirty flagstones. The weapon is primed and ready. He strides through the farmyard and into the field. As if sensing his presence, Damien turns.

"You gave the estate agent an awful fright yesterday," says Damien.

He props the sledge hammer against the galvanised steel gate and wipes his brow.

"I was hunting for the fox that keeps taking my hens."
Damien narrows his eyes.

"I'll do what I have to, to protect my farm," says Luke.
"Only it's not yours. Never was."

Luke entwines stick fingers around the barrel until the only thing that separates him and the shotgun is a film of sweat stagnating in the hollow of his palm. Then he takes a deep breath.

"I've lived and farmed this land with Walter for the last thirty years. That has to count for something."

Damien swats at the bluebottle buzzing around his head.

"Not in the eyes of the law."

Luke stares at him, looking for the boy with the floppy fringe that Walter and he loved. The boy, who ran from his father's farm in the evenings to help them bring the cows in for milking and much later, the man who got the priest to give Walter his last rites as he grew cold in his bed.

Luke couldn't cry at the funeral. It wouldn't do to be seen upset. Walter wouldn't have wanted that. He heard someone whisper, 'shirt-lifter' in the graveyard. That nearly loosened his taut face. He opened his mouth, closed it again and gritted his teeth. Then he grabbed a handful of earth, threw it on the coffin and waited until the last shovel was scattered over Walter's grave.

"Will you come to Mulligans with us? A hot whiskey would warm you up," Damien asked when the gravediggers left.

"What was he doing so close to the pit when the slurry was mixing?"

Damien couldn't answer, just wiped his eyes and the two men's umbrellas leaned against each other as hailstones battered the nylon canopies.

"Nothing will ever warm me again," said Luke.

That night he sat in Walter's armchair in the kitchen, leaned towards the hearth, clutched his ribs and stared into the peat ashes.

"Why did you have to go before me?"

He ruminated until the rooster crowed and brought another December dawn to his door.

He stares at Damien, head addled and doesn't know who to be madder with; Damien for putting the farm up for sale or Walter for not making a will.

"I don't have any rights to this place if anything happened to you," he'd said to Walter, after Damien's father died, suddenly.

What if Walter went the same way as his brother, he wondered as the bed creaked and Walter rolled towards him and took hold of his face.

"Nothing's going to happen. I'm in great health," he said as his lips moved towards Luke's.

Luke felt himself go hard as Walter stroked his chest and played with the knots of hair that covered it.

"I'll look after you. Haven't I always?"

Luke closed his eyes, inhaled his lover's freshly showered body; a hint of manure still lingered on the back of Walter's goose-skinned neck.

Damien checks the stake to see if it's steady, then picks up the sledgehammer and walks towards the Land Rover as if there's nothing more to be said.

"That's not going to stay standing for long," says Luke, raising his shotgun.

Damien shouts over his left shoulder.

"I'll be back tomorrow."

"I don't understand. Why are you doing this?"

Damien turns, stops and kicks at a clump of bulrushes beside him.

"It's my land now."

"What am I supposed to do?"

"Put that gun down for a start."

"Your uncle's heart would be torn in two if he saw that sign," says Luke, trying to still his shaking hand.

"I think he'd understand."

"Well if I don't, how the hell would he?"

The cattle low in the top field. Damien turns to look at them.

"Have you not milked the cows yet this morning?"

"I was just about to when you arrived."

Damien whistles for the sheepdog. She nearly knocks the gun from Luke's hand as she rushes past and mooches around Damien's boots. He stoops to pet her.

"You'll have to sell the cattle, too. There won't be room on your land," says Luke.

Damien stops petting the dog and stands up.

"I know."

Luke can hardly hear his voice. It reminds him of the time Damien told him he'd been bullied in school because of Walter and himself.

Luke had ruffled the auburn hair on Damien's bowed head.

"Pay no heed to them bucks," he'd said.

He knew it wouldn't happen again because he'd be roaming through the fields later that evening hunting foxes and he was sure to happen upon some of those lads and that would be the end of the teasing.

Luke lowers the shotgun, edges closer to Damien and scans his frame. Is there any bit of that boy left in him at all, he wonders. His throat feels raw as he speaks.

"Do you know where I feel closest to him now?"

Damien shrugs.

"At night beside the fire when I'm trying to finish the crossword in the Farmers Journal."

"He was a great man for the crosswords."

"And he loved helping you with your homework."

Damien pulls a bulrush from the nearby clump and winds it around his forefinger.

"I miss him too," he says.

Luke clenches his eyes shut for a minute. He'd managed this far without crying. Sure as hell not going to start now. The horn on the Land Rover beeps. Luke's body shakes and he opens his eyes but all he sees is a watery haze. He drags the sleeve of his shirt across his face and turns his head towards the lane. Then he glances at Damien who stares at the shotgun in his hand.

"Shane's in the jeep."

"Jesus, why didn't you tell me before now?"

"You didn't give me a chance."

The boy pokes his thin face out the passenger window. Luke's shocked by how pale he looks. Almost as white as his father.

"He's still talking about the story you read to him the last time you visited."

Luke shoves the shotgun behind his back.

"*Fantastic Mr. Fox*? I used to love reading the Roald Dahl books to you, too."

"Remember when I used to go hunting foxes with you? Mam nearly had a seizure, when I told her you let me have a shot."

Luke can still hear Damien's whoop of joy when he managed to shoot a crow.

"Aye and you had the finest aim of any young buck in the parish."

"I had a good teacher. Though, I don't remember you ever killing a fox," says Damien.

Luke gets a sudden urge to hug him. Then the sun bounces off the 'For Sale' sign and he shields his eyes from its fiery rays. The shotgun slips out of his hand. He wipes his sweaty palm down the side of his trousers. His right hip cracks as he bends and picks it up. Damien grabs his arm.

5

"I don't want to sell."

"Then why?"

"I have to find some way of paying herself off. She wants a divorce."

"What? Jesus Christ, why didn't you tell me this sooner?"

"We haven't exactly been on speaking terms lately, have we?"

Luke looks down at his mucky boots as he remembers the times he wouldn't answer his mobile when Damien rang. But there's that little voice reminding him of the way his hands shook when he read the solicitor's letter, saying he was entitled to nothing. Luke couldn't bear to talk to Damien then, couldn't believe he would sell his home out from under his feet. He raises his head.

"No, we haven't," he says.

"If I want to keep my own farm I have to buy her out. That's why I have to sell this place."

Luke can't look at him anymore. He turns away.

There's a flash of red, half-way down the field. Instinct propels him to raise the shotgun, aim …

"Luke, don't."

Damien runs towards the Land Rover. Shane's shriek paralyses Luke's finger. His grip slackens and the shotgun lands on the grass. The white tip of the fox's bushy tail disappears into the blackthorn hedge at the bottom of the field. There'll be another time, Luke thinks as he walks towards the jeep where Damien is hugging his son.

"Sorry, I didn't mean to frighten Shane. It's just that I've been after that fox for the last week."

"I thought foxes only come out at night," says Shane.

"You never know when they're going to show up," says Luke, reaching into his trousers pocket and pulling out two euro.

"Here, buy yourself some sweets at the County Show on Sunday."

Damien takes the coin and gives it to Shane.

"Thanks," he says. "Why don't you come with us?"

Luke puts his hands back into his pockets.

"I'd only be in the way."

"I could do with some help to keep an eye on this lad," says Damien as he brushes Shane's fringe out of his eyes.

"You're a great father. He's lucky to have you."

Damien lowers his head and leans towards Luke.

"The house feels so empty without her."

Luke turns and looks at his half-closed back door.

"I know what you mean."

Damien puts his palm on the back of the older man's shoulder.

"You could move in with us."

"I could," says Luke as he takes a step back, walks to where the shotgun lies and picks it up.

"And maybe it's time you gave up hunting foxes."

"Aye, maybe it is."

After his tea Luke throws last week's unfinished Farmers Journal crossword into the fire. He takes the shotgun from where it leans against the corner of the mantelpiece and swats the midges that crowd his face as he steps out into the evening sun. The hens scatter as he walks through them towards the slurry pit. Just as he's about to lift the hatch of the pit he sees his prey, skulking near the door of the hayshed.

Luke's eyes run along the fox's long sleek body, from his bushy tail to his pointed ears. He raises his shotgun, finger sliding over the trigger. He can see the black whiskers on the fox's muzzle twitch but the animal doesn't move.

The hens' clucking turns to squawking until the gunshot silences them and the only sound that Luke hears is the hiss of air escaping from one of his tractor's tyres, then the swish of branches as the fox disappears into the wood of pine trees behind the shed.

"Goodbye, Mr. Fox."

Luke lifts the hatch off the pit, throws his shotgun into the slurry and bangs the hatch shut.

Half-a-Boy

"Mattie, stop. You'll burn the house down," said Mam, prodding me in the back with the poker, the other day.

But there's no heat in the sods anymore, no matter how many I put on the fire and now I'm kicking huge holes in the bank those sods came out of.

"Useless fucking turf."

Maybe it's Grey I should be kicking? For throwing Joe off his back the last time we were going to the bog. Or that big lump of a stone that hit Joe in the head when he fell. Bloody stones. We'd killed ourselves half the summer picking them out of the top field and they still came back. I reckon God does make it rain stones in the middle of the night. He must think we haven't much to be doing except picking stones. But He's wrong; we've lots to be doing.

Joe's in hospital now. The grey brick one on the edge of Castletown. St. Bridget's. That's why I'm walking through the bog today. I'm going to see him and it's much quicker to go the bog-way. I want him to come home before everything falls apart. Sure I wouldn't be here to save turf in the middle of November, would I?

I wish we was saving turf, meself and Joe. We used to have great craic, we did. Jumping off the banks as we swigged tea from whiskey bottles and taking huge chunks out of Mam's soda bread.

"Time for ye to stop being so wild. Ye're nearly men now."

Mam's killed telling us that.

"Old enough to start acting responsibly."

"What does she mean, Joe?"

"We have to stop messing, that's what she means."

I'd do me best to stop messing if he'd come home from hospital. I would.

She got rightly riled the day he fell off Grey. Said it was my fault. If I wasn't cod-acting the horse wouldn't have bolted but that's not the way it was at all. If she'd let me explain I'd have told her that. But no, she believed Fr. Constantine. It was him striding down the lane lifting his bat-wing cassock so it wouldn't dip into the cow shite. That's what frightened old Grey. I'm sure of it.

I was walking alongside the horse with the turf spades in me hands and when I saw Fr. Constantine me fingers let go off them.

"Waving the spades over his head, he was. No wonder the horse jumped," he said to Mam.

I don't remember doing that. All I remember is the blood, splattered all over that stony field and me bawling 'cos I thought Joe was dead on account of him looking so pale.

I'm shivering now and I know I wouldn't be shivering if Joe was here. How long does it take to fix him up?

"Just a bang to the head. He'll be right in no time," said Mam, when she came home from the hospital.

So why is he still there? And anyway St. Bridget's not a real hospital; everyone knows that. They don't keep you long in real hospitals; weeks at the most. It's months he's there and every time I see him it's worse he seems to be getting. He'll hardly talk or make a grunt or anything and his face is all crooked.

"It's the tablets he's on," said Mam, the other day "He needs them for those awful headaches he gets."

It's them tablets that have him the way he is but I can't say that or me cheek will be stinging from the flat of her fingers. And I can't do things as good as he used to. The cows won't stop kicking when I'm trying to milk them. It's me hands. Sure what cow wouldn't kick a buck with cold hands?

I decided today seein' as it's a Sunday and Mam's gone to Mass, I'd go see Joe.

"He has my poor heart broken. He won't even go to Mass anymore. Will you talk to him?" she said to Fr. Constantine last week.

Then she told him what I did to the picture of Jesus and the two robbers on the crosses that's on our bedroom wall. He did talk to me and I told him.

"It's their eyes. They won't stop looking at me when I'm trying to sleep and it wasn't so bad when Joe was in the bed beside me. Some nights when I couldn't sleep he'd throw his shirt over the picture so the two robbers couldn't look at me. But Joe wasn't there the other night nor was his shirt. So I took his ash stick from under the bed, the one he plays hurling with and smashed the picture only to stop those two robbers looking at me, Father."

Of course that's not really true. Joe was in one of me dreams and he told me to smash that bloody picture 'cos he hates the sight of Christ after Him letting *him* fall off Grey. But I couldn't tell the priest that.

Jesus, I have me shoes destroyed from kicking that turf bank. Mam'll kill me if she sees the state of them. Well, no point in trying to clean them now, not till I get out of the bog. There's a fierce black cloud in the sky. I'd better hurry up or I'll get soaked and they mightn't let me past that big green door in St. Bridget's with wet clothes and mucky shoes. Maybe I shouldn't have gone this way at all.

"Would you just stop and think before you do something?"

That's what Mam is always saying.

"He wasn't made for thinking. I do the thinking, he does the doing," Joe used to say.

Then he'd knock Dad's old peak cap off me head, put his hand under me chin and lift me face to make sure I was listening.

"Isn't that right, Mattie?"

But I'm *thinking* now, 'cos Joe's not here to do it for me. And I'm thinking I'm not much use to Mam without him around. And I'm remembering what Fr. Constantine said to her last night;

"Would you consider putting Mattie in St. Bridget's? They'll take him now he's eighteen."

"I don't know if I could bear having the two of them in there," she said.

"He's no use to you here and if he can destroy a picture of Our Lord there's no telling what he might do to you."

"But that was only because he was so upset about Joe and I need a man to work the farm."

"I hate to say this to you, but Mattie will never be a man. He's only half-a-boy, God bless him. You could sell the land."

I wanted to shout:

"Isn't half-a-boy better than no boy?"

But I couldn't 'cos then they'd know I was hiding behind the couch and there'd be fierce trouble altogether.

"Paddy would turn in his grave if I let the farm go."

Me Dad turning in his grave didn't seem to bother Fr. Constantine.

"It'd still be in the family if you sold it to your brother-in-law. I'm looking for a housekeeper. That'd be a much easier life for you."

I know I'd be with Joe if they put me in St. Bridget's but I can't stand the smell there. I hold me nose when I go to see him but I couldn't be doing that for the rest of me life. Once they'd put me in I might never get out. And it's not as if they'd let me sleep with Joe. The matron told me to shush the last time I was there.

"You're upsetting the other patients. They don't like loud noise," she said.

I was only trying to tell Joe about the fox taking the hens and me running after him with Dad's shotgun. Fr. Constantine took that too.

12

And there'd be no jumping on beds or anything like that. All the men in Joe's ward do is drag their legs after them and you should see the big humps of shoulders on them. When you try to talk to them, they'll either keep looking at the floor or else look right through you, as if you weren't standing there in front of them. The worst thing of all is I don't think Joe knows me. He won't even smile when he sees me coming and if he doesn't know me, how can I get him to come home with me?

There's the quarry. I wasn't long getting through the bog after all. I'll get some grass and take the muck off me shoes before I go out to the road. The lake on the floor of the quarry looks awful oily. I wonder what'd be like in there now. Maybe I'd turn into an eel if I dived in. We had one for tea once. Joe caught it in the River Barrow and it was a Friday. You should have seen it jump all over the pan while Mam was trying to cook it.

      I know that lake's quare deep 'cos Joe tried to dive to the bottom of it one day when I threw in a penny that Fr. Constantine gave me on one of his visits. But I couldn't stand the church smell that was on it. You know the smell you get when they wave that thing around at Mass and smoke comes out of it. Fr. Constantine waved it around Dad's coffin and I nearly got sick right there in the front seat of the chapel. But I swallowed it back down again 'cos I knew that I'd get a clip around the ear if me porridge came up and landed all over Fr. Constantine's shiny black shoes.

      "There's no bottom in that lake." Joe said. "That penny's gone straight to Hell."

      "I wouldn't go to Hell. Would I, Joe?"

      "No, boys like you go straight to Heaven."

      The muck won't come off me shoes. No point in going to town in dirty shoes and if I go home Mam'll surely kill me when she sees them or worse, march me straight into St. Bridget's in me bare feet.

Maybe half-a-boy isn't better than no boy.

What'll I do then? I'll climb our tree, that's what I'll do. Though it looks awful sad, bent over as if it's about to jump into the quarry. I love the leaves on it. They have five fingers. But there's no leaves on it today, they're all on the ground and they're the colour of calf scour.

Joe used to hang a rope off one of the branches and we'd swing out over the quarry's edge, roaring our heads off and he'd shout at me:

"Don't let go."

Ropes gone now. I can still climb it. All the way to the top. Out onto the longest branch. Lying down hugging it, I am, and I wish it was Joe I was hugging.

"Let go."

"Why Joe?"

"You want to be free, don't you?"

I'm a monkey. Me arms and legs hanging on to the branch. See how long I can hang with just me arms and now - one hand. See if I can count to ten. The Master used to grip the cane fierce tight when I tried to count for him in school.

Close me eyes. Whatever happens; it'll be God's will, as Fr. Constantine says.

I'm a snipe. No. A hawk.

"Can you see me now, Joe?"

I'm wet and there's an eel with Joe's face and he wraps himself around one of me legs but I don't kick or wave or even breathe. And I'm not half-a-boy anymore. I'm an eel just like Joe and we swim round and round our oily lake.

Demise of the Undertaker's Wife

He looked very solemn in death. Not at all like the Jack that would
be in the pub on a Saturday night buying drink for half the country.
I had a fierce job getting his eyes to stay shut and as for his gaping
mouth. I thought I'd have to put Super Glue on his lips.

It was hard to see a man I went to school with in one of my
coffins even if he had spent all of sixth class kicking me under the
desk when the teacher wasn't looking. Hard to believe that was
over fifty years ago. If we knew when we were young lads how our
lives would turn out, would we have bothered with it, at all?

That's what I was thinking when I was talking to Jack's
father the day before the funeral.

"Will you take cash?" he said, hunching his shoulders and
looking at the oak coffin I'd just shown him.

I had to think for a minute before I answered him. Most
people don't talk about paying until the funeral is over.

"No need to worry about that yet," I said.

"I was keeping the money for my own funeral, for Jack to
bury me. What was the man above thinking when he took him
first?" he said.

I rubbed my hand along the coffin's lid not knowing how to
answer that question.

"Sorry. I've nothing smaller. I'll have some on Friday if
you want to wait."

"No, it a perfect size."

"Perfect?" I said, thinking of Jack's scrawny body.

"Julius and Caesar will fit in nicely, one on each side of
him."

I lifted my hand off the coffin and leaned towards him,
expecting to get the smell of whiskey off his breath.

"Poisoned, they were. Jack was awful depressed after he
found them both dead in the field at the back of the house, the day

before he died. He always said he wanted his dogs buried with him."

I've had some requests in my years at this job, but I have to tell you this beat them all hands down.

"And put the lid on the coffin for the wake. Can't have the neighbours looking at him."

Jack's face had hit concrete when he fell. Or jumped. Not sure exactly and it's not something I'd ask his father. I'd done my best to make him look presentable.

"You won't charge me extra for the dead dogs, will you?"

"God, no."

"Thanks. I don't care what they say about you, but you're a decent skin. You know Jack's heart wasn't able for what he was at. That ghost estate on the edge of town killed him. There was no way he was ever going to sell those houses."

His words fell into an angry silence as he struggled to keep his hard man's face from cracking. A tear sneaked out and hung off the cliff of his cheek bone but I knew better than to touch him.

It must be six months ago since I last touched Maureen. Reached my hand across the space between us in our king-size bed. Under the crumpled sheets. Over her right thigh.

"You don't have to," she said, her stiff back facing me.

Her voice chased away my eager hand. I looked at it for a moment to see what was wrong with it. Then the snooze alarm went off. She didn't move. No gentle shove out of the bed like there used to be. I can't remember how long ago that stopped. I thought maybe she didn't want me near her because of the operation on my prostrate. If that had been it I might have understood.

I couldn't understand why she didn't come to Dublin airport to see our only son off to Canada last month.

"It's a pity your mother couldn't come with us today. Since she got that part-time job with Jack Costello, we hardly ever see each other."

He just hitched his backpack onto his shoulders and tightened the straps around his chest without a word.

"Will they let you bring that bag on the plane?

"It's fine, don't be worrying, Dad."

His eyes darted around the departure area full of other sons and daughters hugging their parents. Then he fixed his gaze on a lad in front of us. A grey-haired woman with fine motherly breasts clung to him crying. It must have triggered something.

"I saw them," he said.

"Saw who?"

"Mam and some man. Didn't get a right look at him. In a black Audi, down by the river."

I wished then that he would just go before I started crying because I was very close to it. He gave me one of those awkward footballer's hugs that he would give his opponent after losing a soccer match. I took the hug and let him go. He didn't look back as he went through the security gate.

I went into the disabled toilet before leaving the airport. Thank God for the roars of all those planes. They hid mine. Then I shuffled my way through the crowds back to the car and drove it home as if I was driving the hearse.

I went to the solicitor the following week. He charged me ninety euro for a ten minute conversation and I was still none the wiser.

"Why would you be thinking about separating?" he asked as he scrawled on his yellow notepad.

"I just want to know where I stand if it were ever to happen. What would she be entitled to?"

"It depends on whether you settle amicably or go to court and then it can depend on the judge."

17

I pushed back the chair I was sitting on, stood and leaned over his teak desk.

"Can you not give me a straight answer?"

He dropped his pen and looked up at me.

"More than likely she'd get half of everything."

The front door of the funeral home slammed as I was about to straighten Jack's tie. Maureen burst into the viewing room.

"What are you doing here?" I said.

"Something's wrong with my Visa card. I was in town this morning, saw a lovely pair of heels and the card got declined."

"I must have forgotten to pay the bill."

"You never forget."

"There's always a first time."

"This isn't funny."

She was about to start one of her rants when she looked to see who was in the coffin. The surface of the rant gave way to tears. She fumbled in her handbag for tissues, the bag with the Guess label on it. Those shoes must have been something, I thought.

"What's Jack doing here? I thought his funeral wasn't till tomorrow. Are they not waking him in the house tonight?"

"No, his father wants it all done as quick as possible. Straight to the church from here this evening."

"What the hell are his two dogs doing in there?" she said, stumbling towards the coffin.

Her tissue wasn't providing much soakage for her tears. She started stroking his tie.

"It's a bit creased," she said, her voice croaking.

She never noticed my creased shirts that lay in the laundry basket for days. I used to end up having to bring them to the launderette. She told me she hated ironing after we got married. Still, she was a great cook, always trying out new recipes. Green

18

curries, red curries, ragus, sweet and sour. You name it, we had it. I never knew what I'd get for dinner, but it was always tasty. I'll miss that.

She started to finger the buttons on his suit jacket.

"Maureen, his family will be here soon. It wouldn't look good for you to be here crying."

"Yes, you're right," she said, bending down to kiss him on the forehead.

"Jesus, Maureen, there's no need for that."

She looked at me and I didn't know what was in her eyes. The fact that they were half closed and still full of tears didn't help. She came over to where I was standing at the other side of the coffin. For a minute I thought she was looking for a hug, and you know, I'd nearly have given her one. Then I remembered our son's words at the airport.

"I saw them in a black Audi."

A black Audi. Jack had a black Audi. Fuck, how could I have forgotten?

"I cancelled the card," I said.

"Why?"

"The bank rang me last week. For the third month in a row you've gone over the credit limit."

"It never seemed to bother you before. Business has never been better. It's not as if you can take it with you when you're in a wooden box like poor Jack."

"I've been checking the Visa statements. Bills for hotels we've never stayed in."

My voice was getting a bit too high for a funeral home. She took her hand off Jack's body and used it to rub her eyes.

"So are you going to tell me who it is?" I asked.

She sneaked a quick look at Jack's face but I caught her.

"It's him, isn't it? Or should I say it *was* him," I said, saliva hitting her in the face as I spit the words out.

"It's over now," she said, turning to walk away.

I grabbed her arm and the blood left her face. I would have frightened myself as much as her with my tight grip only that the picture of her and him in his black Audi was tormenting me. If she had apologised or offered some sort of an excuse, it might have helped calm me down.

"I'm too upset to talk about this now. Anyway I told Jack last week that I couldn't see him anymore," she said, trying to pull her arm from my hand.

"Is that supposed to make everything alright? So what are we supposed to do now? Kiss and make up? Forget this ever happened?"

I was shouting and laughing at the same time but didn't loosen my grip. She didn't answer and to be honest, I don't think it would have done any good if she had.

It's funny but I can never recall what happened next. All I remember was thinking how they were a perfect fit, herself and Jack Costello.

Her warm corpse clung to his, as I screwed on the lid of the coffin. It was a difficult job getting it shut. My heart was thumping and hands shaking. I managed to squeeze the Guess handbag between Jack's shoes.

I had to take the two dead dogs out of the coffin so there'd be enough space for Maureen. The weight of them nearly killed me as I dragged them out back and put them in the boot of my car. I'd bury them in the garden later, under her rosebushes.

I put the photo, Jack's niece had brought in earlier, on the coffin lid and sat down in the chief mourner's chair to clear my dizzy head. The shock of it all ripped through my body like a tornado. I steadied myself, which was no mean feat, given the circumstances. Then I put on my undertaker face, stood up, left the room and locked the funeral home's front door. I badly needed a pint before the wake.

Our Mothers Lied. That's the Truth

The ink from her fountain pen bruised the space between "Mothers" and "lied." Sr. Elizabeth had written the letter three times and was not going to write it again. She wondered if she would ever send it. Folding it into perfect rectangles she put it into an envelope, addressed it to Mother Superior and placed it on the page between the books of Genesis and Exodus in her Bible. Then she locked her bedroom door as fresh air beckoned.

Elizabeth loved the lake at that time of the year with its verges polka-dotted with buttercups. As she walked the breeze tried to smooth out her wrinkling face. She didn't notice the children's laughter, parent's rising voices and barking dogs as she sat on Sr. Teresa's bench. She was glad to be able to sit with her shadow for a while.

She put the earphones of her old Walkman onto her ears. The spools scratched as they turned the ribbons of the cassette tape, scratches that threatened to scar the words of her favourite song, *Only a Woman's Heart*. She'd played it every day since its release, the same week Teresa died. It was only at the lake that she listened to it; only there could she lie in her private mausoleum of grief.

"I mourn for my dreams. I mourn for my wasted…"

The song stopped as the spools screeched to a halt. Elizabeth pressed and pressed the play button but it was too late. Tears stagnated in the corners of her eyes as she remembered a conversation she had with Teresa on another summer's day.

"Maybe we should leave the convent," said Elizabeth.

"Now's not a good time," said Teresa.

"I don't understand. You were the one who wanted to leave, last year. It was you that started this, not me."

"I know, and we've shared so many sacred moments."

"We can have many more. Out there in the real world, where we won't have to feel so guilty."

"We can't," said Teresa, guiding Elizabeth's hand over her left breast. "It's back."

Elizabeth tried to push those memories aside. Years of living with Mother Superior helped subdue the scream within. Light footsteps crept up from behind. Sweet sticky hands covered her eyes. Elizabeth smiled when she heard a familiar laugh.

"Joe, stop, leave Sr. Elizabeth alone," said the boy's mother.

"He's okay. Enjoying the holidays, Joe?"

"Yeah. I want you to be my teacher again next year."

"You have to move into a bigger class and a different teacher," said Elizabeth.

"Aahh."

"You'll still be able to see me. Sorry I can't stay and talk longer but I have to get back to the convent. God bless."

It was getting late and she was on dinner duty. Mother Superior had decreed the evening meal would be cod. Dreary, dry cod. Elizabeth remembered a recipe for a Thai fish curry she had seen in one of Teresa's cookbooks. She decided to cook that for a change. She knew there wouldn't be any fresh chillies in the pantry, so she'd use curry powder instead.

When she got back to St. Joseph's convent, Elizabeth slipped in the back door. Luckily the fish didn't take long to cook. Dinner was on the table in time.

"Where are the Lego bits and other toys? Didn't you say it's a toy curry?" said Sr. Concepta. "I can't eat that. All I can see are bits of white things…fish is it?"

"Cod," said Elizabeth.

"Or maybe it's arsenic. Maybe you're trying to kill me."

23

"Concepta, you know me better than that."

"There's lot of things I thought I knew about you. My model novice and then look what happened."

Elizabeth wished she had called it fish instead of Thai curry.

"Concepta, you're rambling again," said Mother Superior.

Everybody at the table knew Concepta wasn't rambling. Not this time. They could still picture the night Teresa died as they sat around her bed saying the Rosary.

She had reached for Elizabeth's hand. Elizabeth looked at Teresa's face and consequences didn't matter anymore. She held the dying nun's hand and kissed her first on the forehead, then on her lips.

Her actions drew a collective gasp and Mother Superior stormed out of the bedroom. The other nuns followed amidst hurried whispers. Elizabeth lay in the bed beside Teresa, cheeks touching.

"Don't nail yourself to the cross. Promise me you'll leave, find another love," whispered Teresa.

Elizabeth tried hard to swallow the curried fish. Concepta was throwing forkfuls into her mouth, despite the threat of being poisoned.

"I'll give you a bath later, Concepta," she said.

"It's about time someone did."

So, this is my life sentence, Elizabeth thought.

"Elizabeth, I need to talk to you after you've bathed Concepta," said Mother Superior.

"Yes, Mother."

Later, as she lathered Concepta's hair, Elizabeth remembered how the older nun's orange-red fringe used to poke out rebelliously from underneath her veil. She'd always answer Elizabeth's questions with St. Theresa of Avila's advice to pray as if God were absent. *I seem to be doing a lot of that lately*, Elizabeth thought, as she rinsed the older nun's hair. Concepta started to cry. Elizabeth wiped her eyes with a towel thinking that it might be the shampoo. It seemed to help.

It took longer than usual to settle Concepta into bed. As the older nun wandered verbally through convent life during the War of Independence, Elizabeth wondered what Mother Superior wanted to discuss. When Concepta had exhausted herself, Elizabeth left and walked slowly down the long corridor to Mother Superior's office.

"Next time you make a curry, just call it a stew; keep it simple," said her superior when Elizabeth entered the office

"Yes, Mother."

Elizabeth was fed up of stews, but she didn't say that to Mother Superior. Instead she prayed to an absent God for patience and fortitude. The older nun pointed at the chair in front of her big mahogany desk. Elizabeth sat and looked at the woodworm holes on its chunky legs thinking it was time for it to go.

"She's hard work at times," said Mother Superior.

"Pardon?"

"Concepta. It's a full-time job looking after her and some of the others are getting no easier either."

"Yes, Mother."

"We need a full-time carer. The rest of us are exhausted trying to juggle teaching, housework and looking after them. I've noticed a lot of it is falling to you. That's not really fair, is it?"

Elizabeth picked at a wormhole with the edge of her nail as she wondered where the conversation was going. She couldn't detect any concern in Mother Superior's voice.

"Our pupil numbers are falling. We're going to lose a teacher in September. I'd hate to see Miss Haverty go. None of the rest of us are any good at basketball and it was great to see sixth class win the county league for the first time this year."

Elizabeth remembered the furore in May when Miss Haverty had spent a whole Friday afternoon on the basketball court with the school team. Back then Mother Superior couldn't see the point in spending that long outside when there was a curriculum to finish.

"So, Elizabeth, we'll keep her. You can take a break from teaching. You're needed more in the convent. "

Mother Superior got up from behind her desk. Elizabeth tried to stand but couldn't. Concepta would have found it easier to get out of the bath on her own.

"You know how much I love teaching."

"Sarah rang earlier. You can ring her back from here. You're lucky to have such a loving niece."

The mention of Sarah's name pulled Elizabeth out of the chair. She stared at the older nun's straight back as Mother Superior left the office. She noticed a tremor in the woman's left hand as she put it into her habit pocket.

As she walked around the other side of the desk to phone Sarah, she saw the granite stone of the school building through the office window. The evening sun spread across Elizabeth's face, reminding her of the warm glow on Teresa's when they first met.

Elizabeth had been in her classroom all day getting ready for the new Junior Infants when Teresa appeared, eager to look at her new school. Her tanned face seemed oddly out-of-place under the white-trimmed black veil. She smirked as Elizabeth warned her of Mother Superior's dislike of noisy classrooms.

"Huh. She'd never survive in Nigeria. It was great, but it was time for me to come home."

"And I'm glad. Every other nun here is so old."

"I'm glad too. You've got chalk dust all over your face. Here, take this," said Teresa, handing Elizabeth her handkerchief.

Teresa's light touch pushed blood through every vein and artery in Elizabeth's body, through organs and muscles that she forgot existed.

The rest of the summer was lost in lake walks, debates on the meaning of life and moans about their fellow sisters. Then, one evening, in late August, Teresa handed her a letter from a private school in Dublin.

"I don't understand," said Elizabeth, pacing Teresa's bedroom.

"This job offer is a great opportunity."

"You can't leave. I need you."

"Come with me," said Teresa, putting her hands on Elizabeth's shoulders to still her trembling frame.

"But we've only just met."

"I know."

"We're not supposed to…" said Elizabeth, looking at the letter again.

The letter fell on the carpet as lips touched and hands ripped the veil of chastity.

The memory of that night flushed Elizabeth's face. She rested her forehead on the window pane. It seemed as if she had been leaning against the window for days when a voice from behind startled her.

"Elizabeth, you're still here. I think I left my rosary beads behind me."

Elizabeth jumped back from the window, swung to face Mother Superior, her hand brushing against a statue of Our Lady that sat on the edge of Mother Superior's desk. It broke as it hit the oak floorboards. Its owner knelt and placed the pieces on the desk. Elizabeth noticed the tremor in her hand again.

"You expect me to give up my job and stay here looking after the older nuns."

"I'm not expecting you, I'm telling you."

"What if I refuse?"

Mother Superior stood and glared at Elizabeth.

"You don't have a choice."

"I do."

"What are you going to do? Leave?"

"I could stay with Sarah until I get a job in another school."

"That's not going to happen, not if Sarah finds out the truth."

"She already knows."

Elizabeth walked to where Mother Superior stood on the other side of the desk. The older nun retreated, fell onto the chair, took off her glasses and rubbed her eyes. Then she put them back on and straightened her veil with shaking hands.

"Do what you're told and if all goes well, I'll consider recommending you for the school principal's job when I retire next year."

Elizabeth stepped back from Mother Superior and looked towards the office window. She wondered if she could trust her but realised there was no one else in the convent young enough to do the job. *The Principal of St. Angela's National School. Me? There are so many things I could do with the school, with the students, introduce new teaching methods...* The clang of the bell for evening prayer interrupted her thoughts.

Elizabeth didn't go to the oratory to join the other nuns. Instead she walked towards her bedroom stopping first at Concepta's and tip-toed inside. Sleep flattened the creases on the demented nun's face. Elizabeth's ring finger travelled lightly over the older woman's lips. They smirked in response to the touch. Concepta would be the only nun she might miss.

Back in her own bedroom, she lit a Lourdes candle that Teresa had given her. She took the letter she wrote earlier and read it again, lingering over the last three sentences.

"Our Mothers lied. That's the truth. The vow of chastity does not always bring happiness and joy."

She wondered who really wrote those words on the page. Was it the memory of what happened that late August evening with Teresa?

"What have we done?" she'd said, struggling to put her veil on.

"But isn't it wonderful," asked Teresa, reaching for her hand.

"It's contrary to nature, contrary to the Church's doctrine. And what about our vows?"

"Being with you has brought me more happiness than those wretched vows ever could," said Teresa.

Elizabeth had run back to her cell. Shame lashed her skin, leaving welts in the places where Teresa's hands had touched. Yet, she craved for her touch again and again.

Elizabeth still craved for a woman's touch. She knew she always would. She folded the letter again and put it back into its envelope.

I would have been better off if I hadn't broken my vows.

She gazed through the candle's amber flame, imagined the sounds of the school assembly bell, student laughter and her own voice leading the morning prayers. Then she held the envelope to the flame and watched it burn.

WLTM

"How could I live with a woman that buys dogs on DoneDeal?" I ask Frank.

We're in the clubhouse bar. His hip is playing up and he's not fit for traipsing around the golf course. I'm just as glad. It's an awful boring game. He'd suggested we start playing when we both retired, and after teaching together for forty years, I thought I might miss him.

"Kitty's a fine looking woman and it's only two poodles she has," he says.

"I'm allergic."

"To what?"

"Dogs," I say, scratching the back of my neck.

"Didn't your Mary have three of the finest Labradors in the county, God rest her soul," he says.

"Allergies can develop at any age."

So can loneliness, but I don't voice that thought. Instead I shove back my chair and stand.

"And I hear that Kitty's brown soda bread has won prizes," says Frank.

"I'm not going to marry Kitty just because of her bread. Do you want another drink before we go?" I ask.

"Yeah, sure we're in no rush, are we?"

I plonk his chardonnay and my ginger ale on the table when I arrive back from the bar. Frank sits his chin on top of his forefingers and ponders his glass.

"Being on your own doesn't suit you," he says.

I shift in my seat, try to discretely rub yesterday's milk stain off the side of my trousers and wriggle my toes in my three-day-old socks.

"It never did you any harm," I say.

He lifts his gaze from his drink and his eyelids droop.

"True. But lately I'm having this terrible fear of dying at home alone and not being found for days," he says.

"Maybe you should marry Kitty."

"Can't. I'm allergic to brown soda bread."

We throw a laugh into the space between us.

"So what are we to do?" he asks.

Before I can answer the barman turns on the music system and Freddie Mercury belts out of the speakers.

Can anybody find me somebody to love?

The song is still in my head when I get home. I sit down at the kitchen table with a mug of coffee and the *Irish Independent*.

"Go find love, Jim," Mary'd said to me just before she passed away.

"I'd never find another you," I said, squeezing her hand that was more bone than flesh.

She gave me the look she used to give when I'd tell her I'd hoovered the sitting room like she asked but I hadn't.

"You've got a second chance," she said. "Don't waste it."

I used to think Mary and I were happy enough. We didn't argue much. Both of us were busy with our teaching jobs. I spent my spare time either coaching or watching hurling matches. She'd be at home reading her Mills & Boon. Maybe she got from her books what she couldn't get from me.

I put that thought out of my head as I flick through the paper and stop at the Singles page.

The great way to meet that special someone.

I should show this to Frank. Might solve his fear of dying alone. I'm amazed at how people can describe themselves in a few lines. I grab a pencil from the mug on the window-sill. Then I scan some of the words these people looking for love use.

WLTM, retired, well-built, enjoys nights out, sporty, down-to-earth, teetotaller, non-smoker, independent, fit, open-minded, sincere, easy-going, slim.

What words would I use to describe myself? I write in the blank space at the bottom of the page.

GSOH – I always laugh at Frank's jokes so I must have a good sense of humour.

Retired – That sounds better than saying Mid-60s. I could have taken early retirement for all anyone would know.

Well-built – I've no beer gut and my head's in the right place. My heart's in the right place, too. At least I thought it was when I married Mary. She loved me and I thought I could give her what she needed.

Teetoller – That's me and I have a gold Pioneer pin as well for fifty years abstinence. Mary was very proud of me when I was presented with the pin.

Keeps Fit – Yes, don't I play golf once a week?

Enjoys cooking – Mary used to say I should be on MasterChef. But what's the point of getting a load of pots and pans dirty, cooking red-wine sauces and rib-roasts and soufflés for one?

I'm just about to write down *enjoys sport* when I hear the front gate screech. I drop my pencil, close the newspaper and look out the window. Kitty's bicycle is leaning against the front wall and she's striding up the path.

I slink to the floor hoping she hasn't seen me. The doorbell rings. I crawl underneath the kitchen table. It rings again. Shit. Her heels make a right racket on the footpath and then she taps on the kitchen window pane.

"I know you're in there, Jim."

Her tap turns to a rap and the window pane shakes. I feel the beginning of pins and needles in my feet and know that she's not going to leave until she gets an answer. So I crawl out from under the table and go to open the front door.

"Sorry, Kitty, I didn't hear you."

She straightens herself up to her full six feet height and looks down at me.

"Hmh, I only came to give you this," she says, thrusting a loaf of brown soda bread into my hand.

"Thanks."

"You're going to do yourself some serious damage if you keep crawling around your kitchen floor like that."

"I …dropped my pencil."

"Well …I'm off now to meet my new man."

"Oh," I say.

"You're not my type, Jim, no more than I'm yours. The only reason I've been bringing you my brown soda bread is because Mary asked me to keep an eye on you when she died."

"Oh. That was good of her," I reply.

"It was. But I won't have as much time now to be baking bread and calling to see you," she says.

She marches back down the footpath and lifts herself up onto her bicycle.

"Time for you to move on, Jim," she shouts as she pedals down the road.

I put the bread on the table, scrunch the newspaper into a ball and throw it into the bin. Then I stare out the window and decide to go and pull the weeds threatening to strangle Mary's posies.

Later, as I'm waiting for my Marks and Spencer gourmet dinner-for-one to warm up in the oven, the newspaper ball glares at me from the bin. I pluck it from the rubbish and un-scrunch it. Then I open it, turn to the Singles section and look at my pencil scribbles at the bottom of the page.

There's no harm in putting an ad in the paper, is there? But who would I really like to meet? I chew the top of the pencil until the graphite almost poisons me.

When I'm finally finished composing the ad, I phone the 0818 number to place it. The voice at the other end tells me I'll receive my replies directly to my mobile phone. Luckily I still have Mary's old phone, so I use that number. All I have to do now is wait.

"Do you want me to come over and show you how to use the washing machine?" Frank asks the following Wednesday, just as we're about to tee off.

"Why?"

"If I'm not mistaken that's the same jumper you had on last week and - no offence - but there's a bit of a whiff off it. Reminds me of an overdone lamb casserole."

"And what about you and your odd socks?"

Frank pulls up his trousers to examine the purple stripped sock on one foot and the green polka-dotted one on the other.

"I've always worn odd socks, whereas you, my dear friend, have always dressed impeccably. The grunge look doesn't suit you."

I grab a driver from my golf bag and stab a tee into the ground.

"Have you seen Kitty lately?" he asks.

"She's got herself a new man."

"Good for her," he says.

On the third hole Mary's phone vibrates in my pocket. It vibrates again on the eight and on the sixteenth. I'm itching to sneak a look but I don't want Frank to know what I'm at.

"Over par on every hole. What's wrong with you?" he asks, as we load our golf clubs into our respective car boots.

"Sorry, Frank, I can't stay for a drink today. Have a ... dentist appointment."

"At six o clock in the evening? There's no dentist open in town this late."

"I have things I need to do and I mightn't be able to meet you next week," I say, jumping into my car.

As I drive away I look in the rearview mirror to see him bang his car boot down and walk, shoulders slumped, towards the clubhouse. I almost stop the car and turn back but my phone is buzzing again.

Two weeks later I'm on the train to Dublin. I'd gotten nearly twenty responses to my advertisement. Some of them were a bit dubious. Today, I'm meeting one that seems from the text messages we've sent each other to be fairly normal. We've arranged to meet at two under the train timetable display board in Heuston. There's a train at twelve noon that would have got me into Heuston at one-thirty but if it broke down or got delayed I'd be late and who wants to be late on their first date? So I decided to take the early morning train instead.

When I alight from the train, I buy the *Irish Independent* and *Irish Times* and sit in a Café sipping cappuccinos. By one forty-five I've been to the toilet three times, have read both papers back-to-back and completed all the crosswords and sudokus. My handkerchief is soaked with sweat from my palms and my heart is thumping at a fierce rate. I don't know if I should blame the cappuccinos or the prospect of this date. I adjust the black and amber striped tie I said I'd wear and walk towards the display board looking for the wearer of a straw boater hat.

He's there waiting, wearing ... Shit. There couldn't be another man wearing a hat like that. Before I've a chance to hide he's locked eyes on me. My tie is choking me and I loosen it.

For a moment it feels like we could be the clichéd two strangers meeting across a crowded room oblivious to anyone or anything else. But it's impossible to be oblivious to the roar of trains, the loudspeaker announcing arrivals and departures and the screech of wheelie-cases as they're pulled by their owners across the concourse.

Frank walks towards me, looking like he's just won the US Open. I take off my tie and stuff it in my back pocket. Then he's standing in front of me, so close I can smell aftershave radiating from his newly shaven jaw. I look down at his feet and notice two matching socks. He adjusts his hat but doesn't take it off.

"What are you doing here?" I ask.

He puts his hand under my chin and lifts it up so that our eyes are level.

"Same as you, I suspect."

Everything freeze-frames. My eyelids flutter and I've a feeling that I'm looking at Frank in a way I never looked at Mary. I turn and point to the bar at the other end of the concourse.

"C'mon; let's have a drink, I could do with a ginger ale and I think I'll have some brandy with it, too."

French Cream

"Make sure they put the coffin in the sitting room. It's the only decent room in the house, though it needs a good painting. I want it to look respectable for the wake. You'll come with me to Woodies now and give me a hand picking a suitable colour."

It's a statement rather than a request. John doesn't do requests.

"And there'll be no need for this," he says, handing me the letter my solicitor sent him a month ago.

I stuff the letter in my handbag for now and drink the last bit of my expresso. I'm hoping it might clear the muddy head I've on me since yesterday afternoon when I got his text.

Only weeks to live, it said.

And his words when I phoned. "Pancreatic cancer."

The syllables bounced off each other as he spoke.

"When's your next doctor's appointment?" I asked.

"Do you not believe me?"

"Of course I do."

"I want to be waked in the house."

"Have you told your family?"

"You're the first. I don't want anybody else knowing yet."

"You should at least tell your sisters."

"They have enough to be doing."

"Why are you telling me?"

All I could hear for a moment was a crackle on the line.

"I'd like to see you before I ..."

The line crackled again.

"I'll meet you tomorrow morning in O'Brien's for coffee," I said.

Surely, I'd know by the look of him if it was as bad as he said.

O'Brien's is full of black suits. It's just across the road from the county courthouse. The barristers and solicitors are stocking up on caffeine before they do battle for the day. I search John's face as he puts the last bit of bacon into his huge mouth. Nothing wrong with his appetite and he's still built like a bull. He surprises me when he offers to pay. We drive to Woodies. Separately. Meet in the paint aisle.

"So what colour were you thinking of?" I ask.

"Do you remember the name of the colour we used the last time?"

"Taupe."

What kind of a colour is Taupe anyway? It's neither the one thing nor the other. A grey-brown, that's what it is. But it was the on-trend colour around the time of Karen's confirmation.

"Are you sure? It's a good while since you painted it," he says.

"I'm sure. Do you want to paint it the same colour again?"

"Come home, woman, and do it for me."

"What about Courtyard Cream?"

"Didn't we have that in the bedroom, years ago?"

"Or French Cream. It's a warm colour."

"French Cream. I like the sound of that. Might be nice on the chimney breast. And the walls?"

"The same or maybe something lighter."

"I don't know. We'll get tester pots and we can see what's best when we go home," he says, moving closer to me.

The man is as delusional as ever. I hold my breath for a minute. He's full of farm smells. There's dried cow shite on the toes of his black boots. I step back.

"Didn't you say you needed a mirror, too? They're in the next aisle. Have a look and I'll get the tester pots for you."

I watch his long back as he walks down the aisle and I breathe more freely. My head was getting a bit dizzy, probably

38

from scanning the plethora of pots on the shelves before me. The number of different shades of cream paint is unbelievable. I reach up to get at the tester pots on the top shelf. I feel someone's breath on the back of my neck. I turn.

"Christ, I thought you were looking at the mirrors."

I nearly fall into his chest as I teeter on my tower heels. What the hell am I wearing high heels with jeans for anyway?

But if I'm truthful, it's not the heels that I'm mad with myself about. No. It's more the fact that I'm feeling something; something I don't want to feel.

Thankfully my left brain kicks me in the behind. *You can't go kissing this man. Sure, you loved him once, he's the father of your child and he says he has a terminal illness. But remember, you left him for a reason.*

He told me before we'd married that there's something intrinsically sexy about women in high heels.

"It's the way they walk - the gait just begs a man to be there when they fall."

So I started to wear high heels. My bunioned feet have been complaining ever since.

"Can I help ye with anything?"

The gaudy tag on the man's jumper tells me his name is Brad.

"No, thanks all the same."

"We're trying to decide what colour to paint our sitting room," says John.

"*Your* sitting room, not ours."

I put my hands in the back pockets of my jeans and spread my legs to steady myself. Brad gives John a 'sorry for your troubles' look and abandons us. So much for customer service.

"Paddy's sister did it," he says.

"What?"

"She went back to her husband to mind him, after he cut his leg off with the chainsaw."

"More fool her."

He flinches, then drags his fingers across his eyes and up towards his forehead squashing the creases as he goes, almost as if he's on the tractor rolling one of his lumpy fields. He stops and gives me a 'poor me' look. Well, at least that's what I think it is. But I don't study him long enough to know exactly. I look at the tester pots again.

"How can I get you to come home?"

There's a bit of a three-year-old in his voice now.

"You can't."

"I never meant to hurt you. It wasn't you, it was me."

The old cliché again. Christ. He's worse than some of the characters on those rubbish soaps he used to watch; *EastEnders, Corrie*. Of course, his favourite was *Emmerdale*.

"Say something, will you?" he says.

And I'm thinking as he's talking that he should have been an actor instead of a bloody farmer.

I didn't say much the day I left him. Exhausted after my hydraulic screams. Left without a word after what I saw. Well, he's getting his comeuppance now. At least that's what my poor mother would say, if she knew. Not that that's much consolation.

It's quiet this morning in Woodies. You'd think it would be a bit busier for a Friday. Still, I'd better keep my voice down a bit.

"I found you in the milking parlour riding the hired help. How the hell did you think that wouldn't hurt?"

"I didn't think and it only happened the once," he says, looking up and down the aisle.

"Only the once you got caught, you mean. And I don't care if it was a hundred times."

"Look at Hilary Clinton. She stayed with Bill."

"If you were the President of America I might have stayed with you too."

"And she's doing great now. Hilary."

"You never listened when we were married, either."

I lower my voice to a whisper. Wouldn't want to give that Brad fella any ideas. He might be listening to us in the next aisle. He doesn't seem to have much else for doing.

"And at least it was a woman that Bill rode," I said.

We had planned to go to Alicante for a week, just the two of us. One of those second honeymoon thingies that stale couples do. I had great plans. A week of long overdue uninterrupted sex. All packed and ready to go. Me, giving instructions to my sister about what Karen would and wouldn't eat. Him, out in the milking parlour showing the farm relief lad what had to be done. He was a great relief all right.

It ended up Karen and I going on the trip and we stayed there. And no, it wasn't a hot young Spaniard that kept me in Alicante. Nothing kept me there apart from the fact that I couldn't come home and live in that house again.

He has his hands full of tester pots and the fumes from the paint mixer at the end of the aisle make me dizzy.

"Don't bother with all those. They'll just confuse you. Get the Taupe," I say.

"It would be nice to change the colour and we both like the French Cream."

It's a bit late for picking colours that we both like, I'm thinking.

"Stick with what's on it. It's safer."

He puts the tester pots back on the shelf and grabs a bucket of Taupe paint, then pays. We stand inside the exit door watching the rain bounce off the pavement.

"I missed ye. And I thought now that ye're back from Spain, well, there might be some chance."

"I didn't come back for you. I came back so that Karen could finish her schooling here and to get our divorce finalised."

He moves the bucket of paint from one hand to the other. And I'm wondering how a man with six weeks left to live can hold a twelve litre bucket of paint in a single hand for so long. I zip up my rain jacket and pull the hood over my head.

"So I can't convince you," he says.

"Why didn't you come after us when we left?"

"I didn't think you'd stay away so long."

"It's too late now."

I don't look at him when I'm saying that.

"Turning your back on a sick man," he says.

"It wasn't me that had their back turned to you that day in the milking parlour."

He flinches again and walks away, then stops and looks over his shoulder and I'm not sure if it's the rain that's affecting his voice in some way, but it's sounding a bit watery.

"I should have known you'd never come home. Even now that I'm—"

"So, what the hell was all this about?"

The rain stops.

"I'm no good at picking colours. You know that."

He rubs his face with the back of his free arm.

"For God's sake, what are you like?"

He shrugs.

"It really was only the once that it happened. And I've regretted it ever since."

Then he turns and shuffles back to his black Ford Transit van, his head and shoulders descending into nothingness.

Something trickles down the side of my nose and it's not a raindrop.

"Hang on a sec."

I race across the car park. He rolls down the window just as I'm about to knock.

"You're right. A change of colour would be good."

"It's a bit silly to be worrying about what colour to paint the bloody sitting room when I'm dying. I just wanted to make everything okay again," he says, staring out the windscreen, clenching his fingers around the top of the gear stick.

I look at the side of his face and notice how pale his cheeks are. There seems to be a tinge of yellow in the lines around his eyes.

"Go and get the French Cream. Karen and myself might call around when you have the sitting room painted, to see how it looks."

That puts a small bit of colour into his face. As he heads back into Woodies with the Taupe paint, I root through the rubbish in my handbag until I find the solicitor's letter. The wind nearly takes it out of my hand as I open it. I tear it in two and leave it on the dashboard of his van. There's a bit of grit in one of my eyes. I search my handbag for a tissue, then run to my car before it rains again.

Unfinished House

Peter sits on the only chair in his lounge and stares at the Ladbroke website. He scans through the list of horses scheduled to run in the Grand National. *Pythagoras*. A horse with a name like that was sure to win. He logs into his account and enters his password.

The doorbell rings. He ignores it. He runs his hand through his oily hair and glances at the scrunched bank letter on the floor. Thoughts whizz through his head. They wouldn't come on a Saturday, would they? Surely those wankers would give him a bit longer before re-possessing. His phone buzzes. He grabs it.

I'm outside, reads the text message.

He leans his thin frame across the desk, pulls the window blind and sees his mother standing outside. His chest tightens. He coughs to try and loosen it as he drops back into his chair. What's she doing here? He clicks to confirm his bet, closes the laptop then goes to open the front door.

"Mam?"

His mother hunches one of her shoulders to stop the strap of her handbag falling down her arm. Peter scratches the reddening skin on his forearm as he studies her face.

"Are you going to invite me in?" she asks, straightening her pencil skirt.

"What are you doing here?"

She hates the city, almost as much as he loves it. She hates the traffic, noise and smoky air. He looks past her at the silver Yaris sitting in his driveway.

"You haven't been home in months and you hardly ever answer the phone when I ring."

"How did you find the house?"

"Sat Nav, a great invention. I'm giving a speech at a psychotherapist conference in the RDS tomorrow. I thought I'd come a day early and stay with you for the night."

Peter notices she's wearing her therapist face as she speaks. It doesn't stop his mind from liquidising as she steps into the hall, no hint of a wobble in the heels she's wearing.

"Oh, Peter, the cobwebs," she says as he bangs the front door shut.

They drape over the unpainted cornice. A bluebottle has given up his fight to escape and his hunter advances towards him.

"I'm dying for a coffee," she says, marching through the hall towards the kitchen.

"Why didn't you tell me you were coming?"

"I wanted to surprise you."

He follows her into the kitchen and watches her survey the sparse room. Her eyes flitter from the stainless steel sink to the small fridge beside it. Then her gaze settles on the blind-less window and the kettle perched on the window-sill.

"Where's your kitchen?" she asks.

"You're in it."

She scrunches her face. It reminds Peter of a goat. Then she glances at the small table he'd salvaged from the skip at work. She sits on the only chair in the room and drops her handbag onto the dusty laminate floor.

"You can't live in a house without a proper kitchen," she says.

Why the hell not, he asks in his head. He's been living here for the last year without one. When his fiancée called off the wedding, the house didn't matter anymore. Then he and some of his work colleagues had gone to a casino after the staff Christmas party. He'd got lucky on the roulette wheel and at the blackjack table. The skin on the tips of his fingers tingled as he placed his bet. He'd felt himself go hard with the anticipation of a possible win. But he didn't tell any of his colleagues that.

Sex is the farthest thing from Peter's mind as he pulls the fridge door open to look for the Nescafe. Good a place as any to keep the jar, he thinks as he hears her sigh in the background.

"I'll sort out the kitchen when I get a chance," he says.

His mother gives him the look she wears when she's trying to decipher food labels without her reading glasses.

"We could go to IKEA this afternoon and I could help you pick out some nice units."

Peter bangs the coffee jar on the sink's draining board to loosen the granules.

"I've exam scripts to correct today," he says, taking two mugs from the unwashed pile in the sink. He gives them a quick rinse and dries them with a paper towel.

"Do you not have a proper tea-towel?" she asks.

He throws the sodden paper into the sink and glares at her.

"Not that I'm judging," she says and crosses her legs.

Peter grimaces. She claims she never judges. Always spouting that Carl Rogers stuff about *unconditional positive regard*. Even as a boy Peter could see that the words coming out of her mouth didn't always match her face. Maybe in her office with her clients it did. He always thought they got the best of her. Sometimes when he was supposed to be doing his homework he'd sneak out to her office door and listen to the muffled voices.

His pocket vibrates. He digs in, pulls out his phone and swipes his finger across the screen. Then he scans through the race updates. *Pythagoras* has fallen at the first fence. He shoves the phone back into his pocket and scratches the side of his neck. Just as the water in the kettle bubbles, his eyes start to sting. He turns his back on his mother, tips some coffee granules into a mug and fills it with boiling water.

"I've no milk," he says, putting the mug on the table in front of her.

She takes a sip. He wonders if he could get some credit in the casino tomorrow night. He'll be sure to make back his losses at the blackjack table.

"Walnut or cherry?" she asks.

He stares at her.

"What?"

"Which type of wood would you like for the kitchen units?"

"I don't have any money for bloody units."

She sneezes and brown drops of coffee rain onto the table.

"No need to swear, Peter. Surely with the big salary you're on, you can afford a decent kitchen."

He grabs a mug and makes a coffee for himself. Would she show him some *unconditional positive regard* if he told her where his money has gone. He remembers the time he stole an apple from the parish priest's orchard. When she'd caught him eating it, she'd marched him straight over to Father Murphy. The priest gave him three decades of the rosary to recite and his mother banned him from watching television for a week. Peter cried that night and wished his father was still alive. He wouldn't have thought taking an apple was such a huge sin.

He gulps his coffee; it sticks on the root of his tongue. His mother gets up and puts her mug on the draining board patterned with brown stains.

"What are you doing with your money that you can't afford a proper kitchen?" she asks, staring out the window at the concrete block wall that separates his house from the next.

"My teaching hours have been cut. I've been working half-time for the last few months."

"Why didn't you tell me? I could have helped you out."

"I didn't want your help."

She turns to face him. He notices that the lines at the side of her eyes have multiplied since he saw her last.

47

"Have we grown that far apart?" she asks.

He shrugs and her tight face slackens as if there's something softening. But maybe he's imagining it. Still, the lines don't look as deep as they did moments ago and despite everything she is his mother. He remembers what she'd said after his father had died.

"I've taken out a life insurance policy. I want to make sure you're looked after if anything happens to me."

He'd run to his room, crying. At the time it wasn't money he wanted. But now?

"C'mon, I'll show you the rest of the house," he says.

When they reach the top of the stairs she squeezes her nose with her thumb and forefinger.

"What's that awful smell?"

"I don't smell anything," Peter says, pulling the bathroom door shut.

She walks towards his bedroom, then stops. He watches her glance at the single unmade bed, sitting on the unvarnished pitch pine floor and the MDF locker he bought in Argos.

"You really do need some help," she says.

"Why bother with the house? It's not as if I'm going to get married anytime soon."

"Don't shut yourself off because of one failed relationship."

Peter glares at her as he stuffs his hands into the back pockets of his jeans and says,

"there's been more than one failed relationship."

"Some can be repaired. I had a client recently, he reminded me of you."

Peter grunts. The last thing he needs is to hear about one of her bloody clients.

"This particular client lost his mother, when he was twelve. It got me thinking of what it must have been like for you when your father died."

48

Peter takes his hands out of his pockets and clenches the top of the bannister as she moves closer to him.

"A bit late to be thinking of that now," he says.

"I know I wasn't there for you the way I should have been, but I was so busy working trying to pay off the bills your father left behind…"

"Don't blame Dad."

Peter lowers his head and looks down the stairs at the charcoal-coloured tiles below.

"I just want to say sorry for not being the mother you needed."

She reaches out to hug him. He steps back. Then words tumble out of his mouth before he has a chance to censure them.

"Sometimes I used to wish I was one of your clients, just to have one hour with you that you'd sit and listen to me."

"I'm here now," she says, grasping his other hand.

He shakes it loose and drags it through his hair.

"Please … I mightn't have always shown it but I do love you," she says.

"What if I told you I was in debt? Would you love me then?"

He raises his head and sees the expression she used to wear when his father came home from the greyhound track on Friday nights.

"You think I'm like Dad, don't you?"

"You're not, I won't let you…"

"I'm not one of your clients. You can't fix me."

"There's nothing wrong with you. I just want to help you finish this house."

She puts her hand on his shoulder. He lets it rest there, feels the heat of it. Maybe they could finish the house together, he thinks.

"I'm sure you'll get more teaching hours next term. I'll help you out with the bills till then."

Peter paints a smile across his face.

"Thanks, Mam."

Then he feels a dull thud on the floor of his heart and sweat trickles across his palms. He hears the click-clack of a spinning roulette wheel.

"I could go to IKEA tomorrow while you're at your conference," he says. "If you give me some cash, I'll be able to put a deposit on some units if I see anything nice."

She gives him a look he'd often seen her give his father. But he's not his father, he thinks. He'll win tomorrow when he goes to the casino. He's sure of it.

A Bit of Light

I don't hear any birds this morning. That's good. I wouldn't want
to die on a day that might be full of the voices of wrens or cuckoos
or thrushes. Mulligan's rooster starts to crow. Never a need for an
alarm clock in our village.

I don't know what I want for breakfast. I might have one of
those croissants I got in Tesco yesterday. Not great for the
cholesterol but that hardly matters now. The kitchen window-blind
creaks as I pull it up. Grey clouds dress the sky. The willow Paddy
planted on our twenty-fifth wedding anniversary is flailing in the
wind. As I'm waiting for the kettle to boil, the angel Gabriel glares
at me.

"Are you going to light my candle?" he asks.

"Are you going to let me see him again?"

"You will, in time."

"Yeah, but not on this earth," I say, grabbing a cup from the
shelf.

He can be awful annoying at times. He's been standing on
the window-sill since Paddy's funeral. At first I used to light the
candle that he holds in his porcelain hands.

"A bit of light in the darkness," said my sister, when she
gave the angel to me.

A fire hazard more like. I've often been in the car on the
way to town and I'd be wondering if I forgot to blow the bloody
candle out. I'd have to come home again, 'cos there was one time
that I did forget. No use in having a bit of light in the darkness
when your whole house is gone up in flames. Is there?

"I'm not going to light your candle," I say, rinsing my cup
with boiling water.

My cheeks feel flushed and damp from the steam so I grab
the tea towel and sponge my face. I think of Paddy's red cheeks
and his bulging eyes when he'd get cross. It's easier to think of that

51

than his happy face. I mightn't miss him as much if he was one of those husbands who spent half the night slobbering over a pint in the pub, or worse, slobbering over some young one half his age. Or his passing might be a bit easier to bear if he took a fist to me once in a while and I hated the living sight of him.

But I loved every bit of the man: the feel of the hairs on his back as we made love, the grassy smell of him after he'd come in from cutting the silage, the heat of his hand on my thigh as we sat watching the nine o' clock news on the couch. All the coal I heap into the stove does nothing for me and I can't even get warm in the bed. Despite the electric blanket, hot water bottle and winter duvet, there's a chill in my bones that I can't get rid of.

I clench my fingers around the handle of the cup.

"You've no idea what it's like to lose your husband."

"You're right; I don't," says Gabriel.

"Well, the least you could do is show me some compassion."

I managed to get through Paddy's funeral 'cos I'd planned what I was going to do once it was over. But my problem is that sometimes I find it hard to keep my mouth shut so I told my sister what was going through my head. The next thing I know, Doctor McCarthy is in the house and Paddy's coffin still in the front room. Whatever was in the injection he bruised my bum cheek with, it knocked all thoughts of going to the river out of my head for a while. After the injection he put me on Xanax.

"They'll keep you on an even keel," he said.

I stopped taking them weeks ago. Couldn't fit into any of my clothes and I was walking around in a daze the whole time. There's a text message from Sharon waiting for me when I turn on my mobile phone.

Mam r u at home?

Where else would I be?

"You'd better text her back," says Gabriel.

"Not today."

I grab a spoon and press the tea bag against the inside of the cup I've dumped it into. As I lighten the tea with some milk, Gabriel starts nattering again.

"You could do with some company."

"It's not Sharon that I want to talk to."

It wouldn't be fair on Sharon if I was to see her this morning 'cos I'd hate the thought of her at my funeral, turning today over and over in her head and blaming herself, asking if there was something she didn't pick up on. This isn't about her and there's nothing she can do anyway. Grief is a solitary thing. I read that somewhere. I've never read a truer word. She has enough on her hands at the moment looking after Tommy.

"Well, maybe Sharon might want to see you," says Gabriel.

"She doesn't need me. She has her own family now."

"Paddy wouldn't like what you're planning."

"You have no idea what he'd like."

I throw the tea towel over Gabriel's head. That'll take the shine off his face and maybe give me a bit of peace as well. Then I take my tea and croissant and sit on the chair furthest away from the kitchen window.

I'm just about to take a drink when the back door bursts open. In walks Sharon lugging Tommy's car seat and he's bawling his head off. Jesus, he can roar for a three-month-old. The thin screech in his cry nearly cuts my heart in two and turns my thoughts to the brandy I used to put in Sharon's bottle when she was the same way. But she breast feeds. Maybe I should give the brandy to her instead.

I heard on the radio recently that they don't put alcohol in gripe water anymore, so that's not going to do much good. You'd think by now that someone would have invented an app for the phone that could cure a colicky baby. An app like that would make you a millionaire.

Every bit of Sharon's body is drooping. She heaves the car seat onto the table and flops into a chair.

"Colic?"

"That's what the doctor keeps telling me," she says, as she fumbles with the buckle and extracts Tommy.

The poor little mite's body is shaking and his bib is soaked. His fist connects with her eye and now the two of them are roaring their heads off.

I take Tommy and rest his shaking head on my shoulder. My navy dress will be destroyed with his dribble, but sure, what harm? He's stopped crying.

"Drink that," I say to Sharon, pointing at my tea.

She drains the cup, then bites into my croissant and demolishes it.

"I feel like a failure," she says, between sobs, as she wipes the greasy pastry from her lips.

"Every new mother feels that way; it will get better, pet."

"The minute you take him, he stops crying. How the hell do you manage that?"

"Maybe it's his way of telling you to go have a rest."

She has the look now that she used to have as a child when she'd pick the 'Get out of Jail Free Card,' in Monopoly. Then I think of the neat pile of Xanax waiting for me upstairs in the drawer of my bedside locker. Tommy moves his head a bit on my shoulder so I stand, walk around the kitchen and rub his back to soothe him to sleep.

"I've expressed some milk, could you take him … for a small while?"

I hide the feeling of panic that's creeping through me. I've never minded Tommy before. It would be too much trouble she'd say anytime I offered, what with her breastfeeding and all.

I stare at the shrouded Gabriel on the window-sill, picturing the smug grin he's probably wearing on his devout face.

Is this your way of ruining my plans?

The tea towel doesn't prevent him from answering back.

Sharon needs you.

"I was supposed to be going out with some of the women from the active retirement group today," I say to Sharon, watching the convulsive dance her feet are doing under the table.

"Do you have to go?"

I close my eyes for a minute and sink my face into the crook of Tommy's neck. He smells of talcum powder. Wish I could bottle it and keep it on my bedside locker. It might be better than a pile of pills.

The chair scrapes the kitchen tiles as Sharon stands. Then she's beside me and I open my eyes. There's a tremor in her hands as she turns the tap to rinse the cup. The haggard look on her face makes me want to hug her but I don't want to put Tommy down for fear he'll wake. I glance sideways at Gabriel. Then I turn back to look at Sharon and attempt a smile.

"I don't have to go. I'll have much better fun here with Tommy."

"Thanks, Mam."

Tommy wakes almost as soon as she's gone, which is just as well as my shoulder is killing me. I put him back in his car seat and heat the expressed milk in the microwave. If Sharon saw me she'd probably combust but I haven't the energy to put it in the bottle warmer she left behind. And by the sounds of it, I don't think poor Tommy has the patience to wait.

When the bottle's ready I take him out of his car seat and sit on Paddy's rocking chair by the range. He closes his eyes and sucks on the teat. When the milk is gone, he burps the same way Paddy used to after a feed of steak and onions. Then, an almighty whiff and a look of pure relief on his face.

55

I stand with him still in my arms and push the kitchen window open to let in some fresh air. At least Paddy never deteriorated to the stage where I would end up cleaning *his* behind. Tommy's face is alight now and a warm feeling spreads all over my body. Paddy is looking straight out of Tommy's brown eyes. A gust of wind blows the tea towel from Gabriel's face onto the worktop.

"You brought him back to me."

As soon as Tommy's changed, he falls asleep and I put him into his car seat. I don't want him to get a cold from the draught so I close the window but knock Gabriel over in the process. I pick him up and examine him for cracks. Thankfully there's none. But if I didn't know any better I'd swear there's a tear on his cheek.

Angels don't cry, do they? Still, he looks cold, so after I put him back on the window-sill, I light his candle. As I blow out the match an amber hue travels up his chest and lands on his pale face.

Permission Granted

"Where are we going?"

It's not the words, more the way Eileen says them. The May sun that only minutes before hinted of a warm summer that might come this year hides behind a thunderhead.

"Where we always go," I say.

"I don't mean that."

"That's an awful looking cloud over there. We'd better hurry up."

We do our usual loop around the park in silence. Even though we walk a lot quicker than usual it seems to take twice as long. Of course I know what she means. Her love infuses my brittle bones and softens stiff muscles. It's great to be loved again. But to be honest I'm happy with the way things are. In my mind we don't need to go anywhere let alone have a conversation about where we might be going.

"We could go to Pontoon for the weekend if you like. It's about time I brought you and the house is free at the moment," I say.

"We could."

"Great. That's settled then."

She keeps walking in silence, but at least she's still walking with me rather than away. I touch her fingertips with mine and they intertwine, albeit temporarily.

I'll never forget the day I met her. I'm not really one to believe in fate or destiny or that sort of stuff but there was some synchronicity going on that morning.

"I'm collecting for the Marie Keating Foundation," she'd said, when I opened the front door.

I leaned towards her so I could decipher her soft words amidst the ones Lady Gaga was sending down the stairs.

"Not today of all days," I said, thinking of Joan's anniversary Mass that was on later.

She turned to walk away.

"Sorry I didn't mean to be rude. I've an awful headache—teenagers," I said, nodding towards the stairs.

"I had three myself. Boys. All grown up now," she said. "And you?"

"Just the one; a girl, Tara."

The clouds that had been hanging in the sky all morning burst.

"Come in for a minute, until the rain stops. If you don't mind being deafened," I said.

"I'm well used to it."

That was it. Soon we slipped into Saturday nights for dinner and whatever might come after. It was enough for both of us. Or so I thought.

"Myself and Eileen are going to Pontoon at the weekend," I tell Tara, when I get home from our walk.

As usual she doesn't raise her head from her mobile phone.

"Well...if the weather's good. Did you hear me?" I say.

"Yeah....whatever."

Maybe she's delighted to get a break from my shouts when the volume on her wireless speakers rise. She taps her thumb on her phone's screen. Texting her pals about her Dad-free weekend, no doubt. I don't know why I worry so much about her.

She was in a funny mood yesterday after she came back from an obligatory two-day retreat for her Leaving Certificate class.

"We never say 'I love you', Dad."

"But, sure you know I do, Tara....Don't you?"

"It would be nice to hear you say it now and then. Before Mam died, you used to. Every night after my bedtime story."

"Would it stop the arguments, if I did say it?" I ask with a half-laugh.

"Ah...Dad."

A child creeps back into her teenage voice and I instantly regret my joke.

Fathers love their daughters as daughters love their fathers. It's a given, isn't it? Lately it seems that our love is buried deep in arguments over skirts too short and unsuitable boyfriends. I don't see love in the eyes that peer out beneath the hairs of her brown fringe. Her baby curls cowed by a hair straightener bristle with anger. Anger for not telling her – I love her. Is that it? Is that what I should do?

I can't remember what I told Tara on the day of Joan's funeral. All I can remember is a little girl sitting in a Barbie pop-up tent in her bedroom, the one we had bought for her seventh birthday. I tried to coax her downstairs to play with her cousins and have something to eat. Instead she ate sandwiches and drank Coke in her tent. Later as I hoovered the crumbs, the half-eaten sandwiches left behind, I cried for our loss - the only time I cried.

I knock on her bedroom door, on my way to bed.

"Yeah."

She hides her mobile phone under the pillow as I enter. I stop myself from launching into a rant and sit on the edge of her bed.

"I do. Love you."

She throws her arms around me and part of me wishes that I could read her a bedtime story now.

The rest of the week flies by. I had been looking forward and dreading the weekend in equal measure, but standing against the heat of the wood burning stove, it feels good to be home. The smell of the wood dispels the musty odour of a sporadically inhabited house. Two half cups of lukewarm tea stand beside an opened packet of custard creams on the kitchen table. I can hear Eileen upstairs, opening the stiff wardrobe doors. My back aches from chopping wood and carrying her case. I'd forgotten how much stuff a woman packs even if it's only for a weekend.

I go outside to bring in more timber before the sun recedes. There's no teenage music to wreck my head. It's so quiet that I can hear the water lick the walls of the small pier at the bottom of the garden. The smells of the lake air and sap from chopped wood remind me of why I still visit. The hinge on the iron gate that separates garden from lake has been fixed since I was here last.

What would I do without my brother? He tries so hard to keep our childhood home alive, lighting fires to dispel dampness and meeting the German fishermen who occasionally rent the house. I put the excess wood into the shell of the black Morris Minor that guards the gate to Mam's orchard where branches still droop with apples in September.

I come back into the kitchen and the electric shower starts upstairs. The sound of the pump groaning as it churns out water startles me. I picture the stream pouring over Eileen's body as she washes away the journey's grime. A bluebottle fly brushes against my cheek and guilt hits me.

Was it right to bring her here? Is it right to steal from her bed on Saturday nights; to go from lover to father at two in the morning? It was easy at first and she understood. I needed to collect Tara from the nightclub. There didn't have to be awkward conversations about staying the night.

"That smells good," Eileen says when she comes into the kitchen.

She has a knack for saying the right words at the right time. The velvet tone in her voice drapes around my frazzled head. God, I'd really miss her voice.

60

"Re-heating's my specialty."

In the midst of light from tea candles on the table and the half-moon's rays in the night sky, she could be twenty-two instead of fifty-two. Fronds of dark hair dampen the collar of her cream blouse. The vision in front of me is more tempting than the Marks and Spencer dinner in the oven and the smell of her newly-soaped body more appetising.

She chats as we eat. My em's and ah's are timed impeccably and keep the conversation moving. The moon's light is too sharp now so I close the blind.

"Is there any salt?" she asks.

Thankfully there's a container of Saxa in the cupboard that the last group of fishermen left behind. I bang it off the worktop to loosen the granules. She sprinkles it liberally over the poached salmon.

"There's probably enough salt on that already."

She stops sprinkling and looks at the window's closed blind for a moment, then turns her head as if she is about to say something, but doesn't.

"Sorry, Eileen. Tara's a terror for loading salt on her dinner."

"I see."

Her stern tone tells me she doesn't see at all. It tells me in no uncertain terms that I'm eating with an adult not a child or teenager. We finish our meal, clear the table, wash and dry plates, glasses and cutlery in silence. Not the easy silence of a middle-aged couple that have lived half a lifetime together with the minimum of words passing between them and are now oblivious to each other's idiosyncrasies. No, we're in a virginal silence that needs to be broken if we are to survive the weekend. Only I don't know if I can.

"I left my make-up bag in the car."

"I'll get it."

"No, stay. I need some fresh air."

The door creeps shut after her and the woody air tries to sedate me. My eyelids lower and I remember what Tara had said to me, eight summers ago in this kitchen.

"I don't want you to ever get another wife, I don't want another Mammy."

Is that the hook I'm hanging onto now? Or is it the fear of loving and losing again? I don't want another doctor telling me a woman I love has only weeks to live.

The heat that was in the kitchen earlier has left. I open the stove to stoke up the embers. Acrid smoke escapes and fills my lungs. I cough and can't stop. My eyes sting and water. I bang the stove door shut and lean against the worktop, coughing, spluttering and dribbling.

The latch on the back door squeaks and I feel Eileen's eyes run over me as she walks past. She sits at the kitchen table and waits. Somehow I manage to pull myself together. I wonder if her usual equanimity has helped. I turn towards her. She's folding a sodden tissue in her hands meticulously in ever smaller squares as she looks at me. It's a look I haven't seen before. I search her face for reassurance.

"Maybe I want more than you can give," she says.

Silence descends once more. Then my phone beeps and jumps on the worktop. Eileen gets to it first and hands it to me.

"Tara?"

"Yes. I didn't think I'd hear from her all weekend. She's always too busy with her own stuff nowadays."

"They grow up so fast. We only have them on loan. That's what the boys' father used to say to me when they were younger. We need to have our own lives, too."

"Yeah, if they'd let us…"

"…or if we'd let ourselves, Mick."

I turn away to read the text.

Enjoy ure weekend dad luv T

The candles on the table flicker. I open a drawer, get some more and light them. Eileen sits at the table waiting. I step into her circle of heat. It warms me more than the stove or the flames from the candles can. I kneel down and put my arms around her thin waist.

"Tara will be going to college in September. I've always wanted to move back here. Would you come with me?"

"I love you, too," she says, hugging me tightly.

Billy's Rosebush

"That was some fire. It'll take a lot to make the house livable again, miss," says Mr. Griffin.

I look from the charred building to him and notice he's a damn sight better to look at than the house. A big chunk of a man, he fills his jeans and denim shirt in all the right places.

"It was my childhood home ... but maybe it's not worth fixing," I say.

"Don't worry. I'll give you a competitive quote for the repairs. Is it okay for me to take a look inside first?"

"Of course, Mr. Griffin."

"Call me Rory."

"I'll be in the orchard if you need me," I say, pointing to the clump of apple trees surrounded by a granite stone wall at the end of the lawn.

He wants me to call him Rory. Huh. Though, it's a nice enough name, I suppose. Sometimes I give my plants names. They sit on my apartment's kitchen window-sill and look at me when I'm having my breakfast and dinner. There's nobody else to talk to and only the rattle of the window every time a train passes to break the silence.

I take a deep breath when I reach the far corner of the orchard. It's carpeted with the deep pile of a season's growth. But the rosebush is still standing.

That surprised me when I came home to say goodbye to Mother a month ago. I hadn't lived here since I was eighteen. It wasn't a college place that lured me away. Or a fella. The Leaving Certificate exams had been a disaster. So I'd got a job as a cashier in Dunnes Stores in Dublin.

"It's a pity ya didn't make more of yourself," Mother used to say when I'd ring her on a Sunday evening.

I've lost count of the times I've won Employee of the Month, but I don't think I ever told her about those. At least I can't remember if I did. There's lot of things I wish I couldn't remember.

It all came back as I sat beside Mother's bed in the hospice. She lobbed it at me just as she was about to depart and she no longer had to live with it.

"You know that Billy wasn't really your brother," she said, her voice no more than a whisper, like a cat purring.

The heat of her breath burnt my cheeks as I kissed her forehead. Then I stumbled from the hospice room. An hour later as I sat in my car, forehead sore from banging it against the steering wheel, a nurse rang to say my mother had passed away.

In the days following her funeral I thought more of Billy than her. The daisies on the wallpaper drooped as I lay in my childhood bedroom and the reel of scenes I'd canned were now screening in technicolour on the ceiling. I squeezed my eyes shut but it made no difference. Damn her to hell. It had been so much easier to think of Billy as my brother.

I turn my back on the rosebush for a minute and stare at the house through the apple trees. Mr. Griffin is standing outside the back door, head bent over his notebook. How did I think the fire would burn the memories? It's only scorched them at best. I turn and pull at the carpet of grass, brambles and nettles surrounding the rosebush and curse Father for not having the decency to keep this corner tidy after Mother had gotten too sick to do it.

Once I've cleared the weeds, I kneel and rub the tip of my nose on one of the rose's yellow petals. I think of vanilla ice cream

65

as I inhale. A gust of wind comes out of nowhere and a thorn catches the side of my cheek. I pull back and watch the thin stems flail. It's too early in the year for the wind to be blowing the petals away. I reach into my trouser pocket and finger the piece of twine I'd put in there earlier. I knew it would come in useful for something. I'll tie the rose stems together. They'll look tidier and they might stay with me a bit longer.

I didn't want to give Billy a name when he was born. I'm sure if I hadn't, I wouldn't have cried half as much as I did. It was that blasted midwife's fault. She was one of Mother's best friends, which worked out well for both my parents. I remember lying on my single bed in my flowery-wallpapered bedroom looking at the candy floss clouds outside my window. I didn't want to look at the bruised lump the midwife held in her arms. Not even a whimper out of him. She shoved his lukewarm body into my sweaty arms and told me to give him a name.

All I could think was how can I give a scrap of a thing a name? He couldn't be mine, I'd never even felt him in my tummy. In fact, I couldn't fathom how he came out of me at all. He must have come out of someone else, I thought.

"Baby's come way too early," she said. "He's not going to last long, so if you want him to go to heaven, you'd better give him a name."

So I called him Billy. He was never christened, properly. Father wouldn't let Mother call the priest to baptise him before he died. Giving him a name was the worst thing I could have done because as soon as I called him Billy, I started to feel something. I didn't think I would 'cos Billy isn't really a baby's name. I was thinking of a six-year-old when he was in my arms. A little boy out in the lower field kicking football or making forts out of the hay bales in the barn and I could hear my voice calling him for his dinner and giving out for all the dirt lodged under his fingernails.

Mother took him from me after the midwife left. Then Father came into the bedroom.

"Your brother's too small for a proper funeral, we'll bury him at the far end of the orchard," he said, not looking at Billy or me.

I take the twine out of my pocket and wind it around my wrist. It splits my veins in two but I don't feel any pain. I unwind it slowly thinking that if anybody saw me tying the rose stems together they'd probably think I'd gone a bit mad. But I don't want Billy's roses dying before their time.

That's an awful peculiar saying isn't it? Mother always used that line when anyone under seventy died, like Johnny up the road who keeled over in his tractor cab when he was out ploughing one of his huge fields.

She and Father died before their time too. Lung cancer took Mother. And the cigarettes killed Father. A half-dead one fell on the mat lying next to his bed the week after we buried Mother and the night before I was due to go back to Dublin. Highly flammable, it said on the mat's tag, when I bought it for him.

"It'll bring a bit of heat into your bedroom," I'd told him.

I'd cut the tag off before I laid it on the timber floor. Lucky for me my childhood bedroom was downstairs. I managed to get out of the house before the smoke descended.

When I was younger I used to wish my bedroom was upstairs right beside theirs. It might have made some difference. Maybe then Mother would have known what was going on. Or maybe she did know. I never asked. I never wanted to know the answer to that question.

I wasn't going to risk my life to go up to his bedroom when the fire took hold. And the most peculiar thing about it was that

Father never smoked inside the house. But the firemen and Gardaí didn't know that and I sure as hell wasn't going to enlighten them.

It was about a year after Billy died that my mother and I planted the Floribunda Trumpeter in the orchard.

"Ye can't be sowing roses in that corner," said Father.

"We can hardly put a bloody headstone down here, can we?" said Mother.

That shut him up.

If I'd had other babies what I would have called them? Useless question. That was never going to happen. Father said I was too precious to let any man near me. Not too precious for him. I used to wish I was less precious. But after Billy, Father never touched me again. I guess Billy saved me, in a weird sort of way. Once I left home, I never wanted to be called precious by any man again.

Blasted wind. It's blowing drops out of my eyes. I let the twine fall onto the grass and cradle my wet face. Then I hear footsteps. Mr. Griffin clears his throat and I turn to see him fiddling with his notebook.

"Beautiful roses," he says.

He starts nattering as if he's known me for ages. I notice he talks mostly about good things. Like the first bluebell he'd spotted in the spring or the robin he'd seen on Christmas day or the two magpies balancing precariously on his garden fence this morning. The only time he saw one magpie was when his wife died.

As he talks I pick the twine out of the grass and tie the rose stems together.

"You're going to strangle them," he says.

"I'm just trying to protect them from the wind."

"Here, let me do it for you. They need gentle handling."

He tucks his notebook into his back pocket and kneels beside me. The smoky smell of the house clings to him and I cough. He loosens the knot and reties it. The roses look more relaxed now.

"Thanks. What did you say your first name was again?"

"Rory. It's a pity these roses are down here, where nobody can see them. Wouldn't it be nicer if they were near the house? You'd be able to look out at them from your kitchen window."

"Rory is a lovely name."

He moves closer and I can feel his breath on my forehead. I notice the hollows at the bottom of his cheeks. How can a middle aged man have dimples?

"I could transplant this bush for you, if you like."

I pull back from him and stand.

"No. I don't want it moved from here, ever."

"Sorry, I didn't mean to ...," he says, as he rises.

I stand between him and the rosebush.

"My Billy is buried here."

I wait for him to say something but the only sound I hear is the air leaving my body. He covers one of my cold hands with his.

"I could buy some more Floribunda to plant around the front lawn, if I decide to get the house repairs done," I say.

The heat of the late May sun finds its way through the branches of the Bramley apple tree leaning over us. In another few months the branches will be creaking from the weight of tart fruit. I lift my shoulders then let them fall. I wonder who will help me pick the apples in September.

You Want It Darker

Iscariot

He taps on the ceiling of my skull.

"Leave me alone, Iscariot."

I close my eyes and squeeze him into the cell at the back of my head.

"You're beyond redemption," he says.

That's what he keeps telling me and I don't want to believe him.

I hope Maisie's letter comes today. That will silence him. I love the wintergreen smell of her envelopes, the thrill of touching paper she touched, tracing my fingers around her words. I imagine I'm the pen in her hand as she writes, feeling her fingers on my hard, slim body. I still can't believe my luck, that she was one of the people who answered my advertisement in The Village Voice.

"She's given up on you. Can't say I blame her," Iscariot snorts.

"Rubbish. She's been writing every week for the last five years. Isn't she entitled to miss one or even two?"

"Hah. So much for your grand plans if you ever get out of here."

"When. Not. If."

"Do you really think she'll want you?"

She told me I was the only person who really knew her, in a letter last year. She doesn't tell her co-workers how she dances to *Chuck Berry* every morning before work and that she's watched the movie *Blackboard Jungle*, three times.

"They'd laugh if I told them and we're too busy looking after the patients to chat," she said. "And they'd laugh if I told them about my dream of living at the foot of a mountain and waking up in the morning to the sound of a gushing stream."

71

Her brother doesn't even know that she pretended to cry when her father died. I pretended to cry when I killed mine. Of course I haven't told her that. Yet.

"She didn't like your drawing."

"You don't know that, Iscariot."

It took me weeks to get it right though it was worth it and drawing kept Iscariot at bay. My portrait of her was tasteful, I thought. Okay, I've never actually seen her photo. I drew the woman I knew from her words. Her forearms covered the dark-nippled breasts I had imagined.

"If she knew what we're capable of ..."

"Shut the hell up, Iscariot. There's no 'we' anymore."

"I got your picture, thanks," she said in her next letter.

That was it. No other mention and I thought maybe I'd messed everything up. Or maybe she had a boyfriend or husband that she'd never told me about and he'd found the portrait and beat her. That thought had me pulling hairs out of my beard. But she still kept writing.

I drew a picture of her bedroom last week. She likes cotton sheets so I covered her double bed with deep-purple ones, no duvet needed. Her cream body spread across the dark sheets. I keep that picture under my pillow.

I wonder what Mother would think if she could see me drawing pictures.

"Your father would have laughed," says Iscariot.

I think Mother would have loved to know that I'd found something within me that I didn't know I had; something beautiful. Then she'd know that she wasn't insane to love me. She never stopped till the day she died, even though Iscariot took me from her a long time before her coffin was lowered into the grave.

Sometimes the people who write want to know what has me here for so long.

"Self-defence."

That's how I frame it.

"Only losers with nothing else to do write to men like you," says Iscariot.

I go over to the window-sill and study the plastic pieces on my chessboard. Manhattan Bob has me in check and today's the deadline for me to write back and tell him my next move. I don't think I'm going to win this one. He's already taken my rooks and a bishop. I'll get my revenge in the next game. I've to finish reading the 'Republic' today, too, so I can write to Dean and tell him what I thought of it.

"Republic. Hah. It's far from that you were reared," says Iscariot.

Dean's a lecturer who teaches philosophy at Boston University. He's introduced me to the writings of Plato, Aristotle, even Descartes. *I think; therefore I am.* That's what Descartes says.

"You think of me, too," says Iscariot.

"So what?"

"Writing, reading, drawing, playing chess. Waste of time."

What am I supposed to do, curl up in the corner of my cell and wait till they let me out? Nobody comes to visit since Mother died.

Someone jams a key into the lock of my cell door. I spin on my heel and turn my back on the chessboard. Mike pushes open the door, casting a grey shadow on the cell's concrete floor. He coughs as he puts an envelope on my table.

"Just the one letter, today, Bill."

"Thanks, that cough of yours is getting worse," I say.

He takes a tissue from his pocket and wipes his mouth.

"Yeah, that's what the wife keeps saying."

"You should go see a doctor."

"She says that too. Says it'll kill me yet. But it's hard to kill a bad thing, eh, Bill."

"I guess that's why we're both still here," I say.

73

As soon as the door bangs behind him, I grab the envelope, turn it over to see if it has Maisie's navy fountain pen lettering that always leans to the left. It's an envelope like the kind she uses, only bigger and the letters are straight, no softness in them at all.

Bloody post, it can be damn slow sometimes.

I throw the envelope on the bed. I'll open it later. Back to my chessboard. If I move my king to the left, Bob will take my queen. But I don't think I have any other option.

I wipe my forehead and rub the damp hand in my beard. I can feel the envelope glaring at my hunched back. Who could it be from? Don't recognise the handwriting.

"Open it," says Iscariot.

Without further thought I move my king to the left and abandon the chessboard. The mattress dips as I sit. I tear open the envelope. Out it falls. A faint flutter, then a square lands on my knees. I unfold it, recognising the anaemic blue paper. Catch my breath. I place the drawing on my pillow and read the letter accompanying it.

Dear Mr. Creighton
Aunt Maisie specifically requested that this portrait be sent back to you on her demise.

Demise? Fuck.

She had a lovely death.

Is this guy for real? Some sort of sick joke. I throw the letter on the bed and dig my knuckles into my eyes. My abdominal muscles clench. She couldn't be dead. She's too young. Maybe it's Iscariot playing with the words that my eyes are sending to my brain. I grab the letter again.

She passed away peacefully in her sleep. The way we'd all like to go at that age.

"That age?"

Iscariot does his Dracula laugh.

"You fool, she was only a young one in your head."

She lived a long and happy life and loved getting your letters. It brightened her days in the nursing home.

Nursing home?

But ... she lived in an apartment near Harlem. The heavy air in the summer made her want to strip naked and lie in a cold bath every evening. And I'd be there sitting on the edge, holding her towel.

You are quite an artist. Your portrait showed my aunt in a way I'd never seen her before. A bit disconcerting, perhaps. But then I don't think I ever really knew her. I don't think anyone did.

The letter helicopters to the floor. I jump off the bed and pace from window to cell door and back again.

No ... No ...NO

I bang my fist on the window-sill, send the chess pieces flying. The sound of metal grinding against metal reverberates around the cell as the key turns in the lock again.

"Dinner," says Mike.

I take the plastic tray and the cell door slams shut. I put it on my table, lift the plate's lid. More fat than meat, more water than gravy. I grab the spoon and dig in. Gristle catches in the back of my throat. I cough but can't clear it. The spoon bounces off the floor. I rush towards the toilet and heave.

I take the letter from the floor, scrunch it into a jagged ball, use it to wipe my lips and drop it on my stewed bile in the toilet bowl. Then I kneel beside the toilet and rest my forehead on its lip.

"You thick fuck, falling for her," says Iscariot.

He's all that's in my head now. I stay kneeling until the thud of Mike's boots approach my cell door again.

"Time for some exercise," he says.

I stare past him and walk. He closes my cell door, wheezing. The cigarettes will kill him yet. Iscariot laughs again.

"Who cares what happens to the screw? You've gone soft."

75

I look at the pavement-grey sky as I step into the yard. The bloodied smell of dying cattle from the neighbouring abattoir pervades the compound air. I close my eyes and inhale. I'm a child sucking in the smell of candy floss at a circus. Hold it in my nose and taste it in my mouth. I imagine the rip of a butcher's knife as it pierces the animals hide, their throats torn and arteries emptying warm blood onto the concrete floor of the slaughtering house. I got my taste for killing in that abattoir. Started work there when I was sixteen. But I didn't leave my work behind when I finished and it wasn't animals that Iscariot used my knife on.

"Aahh, the sweet and sour smell of death."

Iscariot's voice electrifies my hair. I feel the roots, pulled straight from my crown all the way down the back of my skull. My eyes shoot open. I stare at Mike leaning against the wall, his jaundiced thumb and forefinger struggle with his cigarette lighter. Click, click. No flame. Click again. I walk towards the far end of the yard, pounding the concrete.

"Christ, that screw is irritating. Can't even light a bloody cigarette," says Iscariot.

I stick my fingers into my mouth, bear down on the flesh surrounding my nails. The smouldering fire on the floor of my stomach ignites. It spreads through every abdominal muscle then to up to my chest and throat. Iscariot sledgehammers on the inside of my skull.

I can't bear it any longer. My body turns, propels itself towards Mike and lunges. He falls and I'm on top of him, punching his stomach and head. Whistles echo in the background, my fist punches harder. Footsteps close in behind me but there's no stopping Iscariot. He can't stop, he'll never stop. Not as long as there's breath in my body.

Mike's chest rattles and his dying eyes catch mine as multiple arms grab me and I'm flung on the concrete beside him. A boot lodges under my left rib. Another, under my right. Dagger pains stab my lungs. I whisper.

"Check … mate."

I clench my eyes shut and stop breathing. Mute velvet darkness descends.

Then I jerk, stung by Iscariot's waspy tone.

"The game's not over yet."

Inside

The wire mesh creaks. Instinctively I raise my hand and peer through crooked fingers to see the mattress above bulging through diamond-shaped gaps in the mesh as the man in the top bunk shifts his weight. I pull the duvet tight around my body, turn over and bury my face in the pillow silently begging for sleep. The mid-morning sun lights the hostel room and I feel as if I haven't slept all night. Then my dream comes back to me – I'm inside.

Flatulence imbued with what smells like cheap whiskey find its way down from the man. I pinch my nose and try to breathe through my mouth. Remnants of acrid nicotine hit the back of my throat. I cough green phlegm into the pillow.

The man's snores stop in tandem with his heavy breathing and I pray he won't inhale again. He does. This time it's faster, rhythmical breaths and the wire mesh screeches as he jerks. The frame of the bunk bed shakes and I wonder if my ex-cell mate is having his morning wank. His daily ritual never bothered me.

Eventually the masturbating man above me expels an orgasmic grunt and starts snoring again. Afraid to get out of bed for fear he'll wake and I'd have to talk to him, I sneak yesterday's *Independent* from under my pillow. The crosswords were great for occupying my mind when I was in prison. I hope they'll give me some comfort now. The other two bunk beds in the room are empty. Their occupants left for breakfast an hour ago. I was glad of that.

I doodle with my pencil on the bottom of the page as I read the clue for two down. Another word for *entrenched* beginning with *I?* Easy - *Institutionalised.* I never need to use a dictionary when doing crosswords. The odd time a word doesn't come to me, I have my biscuit tin. It's safely stored in my grey backpack. Years of crosswords lie there. That's all I have from my time in prison –

an Afternoon Tea biscuit tin of pages with black and white squares. The white ones filled with carefully penned letters in black ink.

The probation officer had told me when she left me at the hostel that she would call in a few days to go through my long-term accommodation and employment options.

"It's a good time to be released," she'd said.

"Is it?"

"There's no need to look so worried."

"Right."

"It's not that bad, Clem. There are jobs out there, if you're not too fussy."

"Fussy? Who's going to employ a middle-aged ex-prisoner? Would you want me cleaning your office or washing dishes in your restaurant?"

"We'll get you something."

I hope she doesn't call to see me too soon. Her high-pitched voice is irritating and she talks too fast. I don't know what type of perfume she wears but whatever it is, it's too strong. Something about her unnerves me. Maybe it's her warm handshake and the feel of her youthful exuberance? Perhaps she reminds me of the daughter I never got to have or the woman I never got to marry?

"No woman will ever have you, if you keep drinking like that," Ma said to me on the night of my thirtieth birthday.

"Ah, Ma."

"It will be the ruination of you."

"Leave him alone, woman. He's harmless," Da said. "He'll find someone in his own time."

She was right, of course. Aren't mother's always right? It hadn't taken much to turn the harmless drunk into a battering machine. A slagging and a shove that knocked a bag of chips out of my hands. Then, three shots of Jameson's and five pints of

79

Heineken took away someone else's son. I knew how cross Ma would be when she found out. As I punched I could hear her crying and telling me how I had let her down but I was powerless to stop the beating I gave the north-side punk.

It's hard to believe that it's eight years since Da died and six since I got the call to say Ma had passed. I hadn't requested permission from the governor to be allowed out to attend the funerals. It would have been too hard for the family to have me standing handcuffed to a guard by the grave. Mam was awful particular about how things looked. There would have been no mad rush by anyone to sympathise with me. I knew that I was as well-off not to be at either of the funerals.

Crossword finished, I have the sudden urge to wash the dirty room from my body. The communal showers stopped pumping almost an hour ago, so I know it's safe. I want to stand anonymously, close my eyes and drown in a spray of warm water. I had always closed my eyes when showering in prison. Unlike some of the inmates, I never worried about what might come behind me.

After the shower I throw on the clothes I neatly placed on the chair beside my bed last night. It's too late for breakfast but I'm not hungry. Though, the smell of alcohol in the room has put a thirst on me. I leave the hostel, head bent and my eyes looking at my feet. Lidl is just across the road. I leave it with a bottle of German wine and a small bunch of blue Irises. They were Ma's favourite flowers.

I haven't drunk since the night of the fatal row. It was my last promise to her. The Lidl wine will be pure shite. And I'm not supposed to drink while I'm on parole. Still the odd slug on the way to the cemetery will do no harm. I've no money left for the bus. Not to worry, Glasnevin isn't far from the hostel and I could do with the exercise.

I reach the entrance to the graveyard sooner than expected. I lean against the open gates and wipe my brow. The walk has winded me and the straps of the backpack are burning the tops of my shoulders. The place looks a lot bigger than the last time I was there, when Ma's Da had died. I pause to look at the grey tower that stands near O'Connell's grave and remember playing marbles behind it with my brothers while Grandad's coffin was covered with earth. I was the youngest in the family and never won a game. Still, no matter how often they beat me at home, my brothers always looked after me outside. Well, they did until they both immigrated to Australia, leaving the family stain behind.

I remember the day one of the prison guards gave me my release date. I knew there would be no one on the outside to look out for me when I got out.

"I'm as well-off to stay where I am."

"Yah big eejit, Clem. Don't worry, there's a pre-release programme. It'll help."

The guard's words hadn't eased my fears and neither had the pre-release programme.

Two grave diggers nod at me as I wander through the maze of plots. My parents are buried in the same one as Ma's family but I'm in no rush to get there. The day's long enough. The noise from the city's traffic fades as I go deeper into the graveyard. I breathe easier now. The city's smog seems to have stayed at the cemetery gates.

A Celtic stone cross guards the family plot. Acned with moss, it's still imposing. It seems to be as big as it was when I was a boy. Aren't things supposed to look smaller as you get older? The row at home when Ma had it erected went on for days. Da thought it was a complete waste of money. A smaller one would have done.

I shiver in its shadow and throw my backpack on the ground. The bottle of wine is empty but it hasn't lightened the load. I kneel and prop the Irises against the bottom of the cross. Ma wouldn't have liked the look of the blue flowers against the green moss.

"Not a bad day for September."

I stand and turn to see who's spoken.

The owner of the September voice is an elderly woman. Her silver hair is tied in a bun. She wears a black wool coat and stands at the end of the family plot, leaning towards the ground, like a weeping birch.

"My Jim's buried here," she says, pointing to the grave on my left. "I've been coming here for five years and this is the first time I've ever seen anyone at this grave."

"I live in Australia – just back for a holiday," I say.

I don't know why I feel the need to explain. I could pretend not to hear her. That was my specialty. I had survived ten years in prison by keeping my ears and eyes closed when circumstances demanded. Maybe it's because I haven't spoken to anybody all morning.

"Isn't it lovely and peaceful here away from the noise of the city? I'm from West Cork myself, but I've lived in Dublin most of my life. I never really liked it, but sure this is where Jim wanted to live."

She edges towards me along the strip of grass separating the two family plots. I watch her carefully for fear she might trip.

"For a place with so many people, Dublin can be an awful lonely place to live," she says.

"That's for sure."

"And it wouldn't be so bad if Jim and I had had some children. I'd have some company, but that wasn't to be."

"That's a shame."

"It is and my only sister died last year, God rest her soul. My parents are long gone. So it's just me now. What about yourself?"

"Just me, too." I say, looking into her face. I rest my gaze on her cheekbones.

"Do you like it, then?"

"Like what?"

"Australia. I don't think I could stand the heat, myself."

"It's not the worst place you could be."

"I suppose not, and ye wouldn't have the same cold or damp that we have here. The dampness is a killer."

I nod in agreement. She's not the worst woman I've ever met and we have something in common. We have nobody. Nobody to love, miss or grieve us.

It wouldn't be such a terrible thing. Would it? I don't know where the thought comes from. Maybe it's the wine. But this could be the perfect solution. Then there'll be no loneliness for either of us. As the plan takes shape in my head, I can taste the sourness of the cheap wine on my tongue.

"Will we kneel and say a prayer together?" I ask.

We settle quickly into a litany of Our Fathers and Hail Marys. Half-way through the rosary's second decade, I stand.

"Arthritis, my knees are killing me." I say, by way of explanation.

The woman pauses and looks up at me for a minute as if she's trying to decide whether she will stand too. She doesn't. Three Hail Marys into the third decade, I move behind her and blow an autumn leaf from her hair. She inclines her head towards me, as if welcoming a strange man's breath. I inhale deeply trying to figure out what the familiar smell is. Then it comes to me: it's Ma's favourite perfume. She's wearing Ma's perfume.

The sky starts to cry as I lower my hands. The vertebrae in her neck whimper as they crack. She slumps and I hold her as she grows cold and stiff. I tidy the grey wisps of hair that escaped from her bun when her neck twisted. Then I lay her out as reverently as any undertaker would, on the roof of her husband's grave.

I borrow one of Ma's blue Irises and put it between the woman's hands and fold them across her chest. Then I kneel and pray for her, for Ma and myself. That's where the grave diggers find me and it's not long before I am back where I belong. Inside.

Author Biography

Anne Walsh Donnelly lives in the west of Ireland with her two teenage children. Originally from Carlow she moved to Mayo, twenty-four years ago. She works as a Student Services Officer in a third-level college and writes in her spare time. Anne took up writing in her forties and it has become a compulsion. She needs to write as much as she needs to breathe.

Her fiction and poetry has appeared in several publications including The Irish Times, Cránnog, Boyne Berries, The Blue Nib and Writers Forum.

Her short stories have been shortlisted in many competitions including the Over the Edge New Writer of the Year Award, (2014, 2016), the Fish International Prize (2015) and the RTÉ Radio One Frances Mac Manus competition (2014 & 2015). She won the 2018 Over the Edge Fiction Slam.

Her poems were highly commended in the Over the Edge New Writer of the Year Award (2017 & 2018). She won the Winter/ Spring 2017/2018 Blue Nib poetry chapbook competition and was also nominated for the Hennessy Literary Award in 2019 and selected for the Poetry Ireland Introductions Series 2019.

She is the author of the poetry chapbook, "The Woman With An Owl Tattoo," published by Fly on the Wall press, which is an intimate reflection on her journey of self-discovery and acceptance of her sexual identity in mid-life.

Find out more about Anne Walsh Donnelly at her website

Website: annewalshdonnelly.com

Twitter: @AnneWDonnelly
Facebook: AnneWalshDonnelly

Other Great titles from The Blue Nib

Dominic Fisher's stunning first collection *The Ladies and Gentlemen of the Dead.* This collection of poems explores ways the living and the dead meet – for lunch, in an artwork, on an allotment plot, in the city. We meet poets, artists and others engaged in the struggles and contradictions of their own times, and encounter challenges from our own.

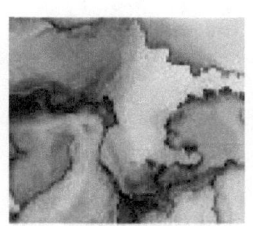

The Blue Nib Chapbook II, also featuring the work of Anne Walsh Donnelly, plus poetry by Dr. Akshya Pawasker, and Bobbie Sparrow.

Reviews for Chapbook II

"I can't say well enough how very impressed I am with the writing of first-place winner Anne Walsh Donnelly who gives voice to her native Ireland like many of the great Irish masters. Donnelly's a rising star to follow."

Find more great titles at www.thebluenib.com

www.ingramcontent.com/pod-product-compliance
Lightning Source LLC
Chambersburg PA
CBHW030538180626
46810CB00005B/1923